When I pulled into Lisa's driveway it was obvious something was wrong. Her front door was slowly swinging back and forth on one hinge, squeaking in the slight breeze.

I got out slowly, eased my door shut but didn't fully close it so I wouldn't wake up my sleeping passengers, and took a few steps toward the porch.

I crossed the wooden planks until I stood in front of the open doorway and saw what I can only describe as what I think it looks like after a tornado hits a house. It was completely trashed; I was freaked out.

I fumbled with my phone trying to dial Mase as quickly as I could. I wanted him to be here when the police showed up.

"Get back in the car right now," he said. "I mean it, now. Lock the doors and wait for me. I'll call the police."

South of the Mason-Dixon Line

by

Kim Chosie

Down South Series, Book 1

South of the Mason-Dixon Line

Cover Art by *Tina Lynn Stout*

The Wild Rose Press, Inc.
PO Box 708
Adams Basin, NY 14410-0708
Visit us at www.thewildrosepress.com

Publishing History
First Edition, 2024
Trade Paperback ISBN 978-1-5092-5252-7
Digital ISBN 978-1-5092-5253-4

Down South Series, Book 1
Published in the United States of America

Dedication

To my people: My Sexy Man, Carmen, Elligrace and Libby.

Prologue

That day, *the* day, started out like any other Sunday during football season with Junior and his buddies getting drunk at the house and watching a game. Zoey was just a toddler and sleeping soundly in her room upstairs. By the time the game was over, his friends were trashed as usual, and despite my efforts to keep them from driving, they left with plans to meet at a local bar. I was too tired to argue with them and went upstairs to take a shower.

This beating was worse than the others.

"Who do you think you are embarrassing me in front of my friends?"

I learned early on that any attempt to explain would just make it worse, so I tried to prepare for what I knew was coming.

This time he broke my ribs and the more I fought the harder he hit me, until he finally passed out, drunk at the top of the stairs. I could barely move and one of my eyes was swollen shut. I knew I had to get out or he would kill me, if not that night, then some other random night in the future, and I had to get Zoey. I thought I was safe as I crept over his passed-out body, mine aching with each step. I moved as quietly as I could and reached for the knob to Z's bedroom door. But he woke up before I could get to her and resumed the beating, spewing words that are burned into my brain. And then it happened.

Something inside me snapped and I became very calm. I felt like I was floating above my body as I watched myself kick him in the chest and reached for the loaded shotgun he kept underneath the bed. I dragged it toward me, slowly pulling myself to my feet, and turned to face him.

"I'm gonna kick your ass for pointing a gun at me," he said, and he lunged forward. I shot him before he took his second step. The house shook with a thundering echo. It was like I was watching in slow motion as he fell to the floor with a deadening thud. I was brought back to reality by the sound of Zoey whimpering from her crib. I never thought to call thought to call the police. I just did what I always did whenever I had a life crisis and rotely called Lisa. She and Ad came immediately, and I explained what happened, emotionless, like I was discussing the price of milk at the grocery store. Ad made a few calls, including to the police, and the ambulance came and they carried Junior out of our house on a stretcher with a sheet over his head. After whispering a few words to Leese, Ad left us alone, and oddly, though I didn't think about it at the time, no one said a word to me.

Chapter 1

Five Years Later

Zoey and I faced each other, and I bent over so that we were eye to eye.

"Left to right, right to left," we said in unison as we rolled the color across our lips. "Rub, rub, cheese." We gave each other a wide, toothy grin to make sure there was no excess gloss on our teeth. Rule number one. It was a ritual Zoey and I began after that terrible winter night that changed our lives forever. It was our protective shield and made us, well me, feel less vulnerable and more confident whenever we began a new adventure. Fortunately, Z was open to this adventure right from the beginning.

"Aunt Lisa wants us to move to Clarksville, you know, in Florida" I had said. "She thinks it will be good a change for us, and she misses us. Thoughts?"

I hoped she would be happy about it because I needed to get away from that night. From him. And he was everywhere.

"I think you mean Banjoland," she responded casually, using the nickname Lisa and I had given rural Clarksville when Lisa and her husband Adam first left New York to head to the deep South, while she rummaged through her dresser drawers inspecting her options. "What does one wear when one travels to the

3

South, Mom? I want to make a good impression."

"One wears whatever one wants, and you always make a good impression, Love."

My body relaxed as I literally felt the stress lift from me—relieved and hopeful for the first time in forever.

She pondered this for a moment. "Okay, good," she said and skipped off down the hall, "I'm going to see what Banjoland looks like on Google Earth."

Sometimes I wondered if she was seven or twenty-seven.

****

And now we were here. In Banjoland, where Lisa and her husband Adam moved as part of his political advancement plan–known to us as "the plan".

"Ready?"

Zoey took my hand as we descended from the plane and made our way over the blistering pavement toward the terminal building because the airport was very small and there was no walkway. The air was stifling and so humid I felt like I was wearing a pair of long underwear in August. My entire body began to sweat and my hair was huge. Voluminous. And poor Z, her normally neat, sleek red ponytail had been replaced by a burning bush of humidity curls. She looked like Annie on a bus tour through the rural south. Weather in New York was nothing like this. We had four distinct seasons and none were called inferno.

Lisa was waiting for us at the baggage terminal.

"Aunt Leese!" Zoey chirped and went running into her arms.

"Baby girl!" Lisa picked up my child and hugged her hard. "I love what you've done with your new do. Vintage Annie." She laughed and ran her fingers through

Zoey's auburn bouffe.

The second I saw my sweet friend I realized how much I missed her. She was almost six months pregnant and was as beautiful as always, but something was different besides her baby bump. She was wearing camouflage overalls...with flip-flops. And her formerly expertly highlighted and glossed chestnut curls were now pulled through the back end of a baseball cap that said, "Bullet Bob's Discount Ammo."

"So, I look a little different than the last time you saw me, huh Mel?" (she was the only one who called me that, short for Melanie. Everyone else called me Lanie)." She snorted that laugh that told me she knew what I was thinking as I took in her new persona with shock and awe. We fell into each other's arms and I knew then that everything would be okay, and maybe now the nightmares would finally stop.

Lisa left the terminal to get her vehicle while Z and I waited for our luggage. It was hotter in the terminal than it was outside. I almost couldn't take it. There was a large man standing next to the luggage carousel who was wearing jean overalls with one side unstrapped revealing a sweat-stained Florida Gators t-shirt. He was dabbing the sweat off his forehead with a torn camouflage handkerchief in one hand and holding a beer in the other. "It's five o'clock somewhere," the man with the Gator shirt said, catching my glance at the beer in his hand as he took another swallow. It was at this moment that I lost any trepidation about moving to a place so rural and different than SoHo, and realized I had to truly embrace this experience. If my goal was to start over and erase the memory of what happened, what better way than in a completely new surrounding? Bring on the adventure! Besides, if Lisa could have a life here, albeit because of *the plan* and Adam's assignment to work with Senator Downes "in sunny Florida" as he pitched it to her, then I could do it, too. Plus, Tallahassee, the capital where Adam worked, was a *city,* and only thirty minutes away from rural Clarksville.

And then Lisa pulled up in a pick-up truck. With a gun rack holding a shotgun.

"Nice rack," I said, smiling and laughing to myself at the thought of my former sportscar driving bestie riding the country roads in a pick-up truck. I avoided the barrel of the gun and plopped down on the seat next to her. And I thought, *when in Rome*, as Lisa pulled out onto the county highway.

We continued to drive along worn, two-lane roads chatting happily, discussing hair products (need to control frizz) and Disney World (five hours away). Then unexpectedly, Zoey blurted out "So, Aunt Lisa, did you know my dad died?"

My stomach tightened and my heart skipped a beat. Every time his name was mentioned I felt like my world was going to implode.

"I did, honey, and I'm so sorry about that (she wasn't). How are you doing?"

"I'm fine, I guess," she said thoughtfully. "I miss him. . ." and then she looked sheepishly at me, "is that okay?"

She hadn't talked about him much lately, and for that I was relieved. She was a toddler when he died so I think sometimes she missed having a father, not necessarily him.

"It's okay, Z, he was your daddy and he loved you, of course it's okay that you miss him."

I am going to have to tell her the truth one day.

She seemed comforted by that and resumed chatting about the abundance of farm animals we saw along our journey, but I was immediately transported back to that night when everything changed. My thoughts were interrupted when Lisa slammed on her brakes and hit the horn. At the same time, I reached across the seat to stop her from hitting the steering wheel, a learned mother's response.

What the...

Outside, I saw the answer to my unspoken question. A teenager driving a tractor had turned in front of us onto Main Street.

"I forgot," Lisa said. "It's drive-your-tractor-to-school day." She waved to the boy on the tractor, and he promptly waved back.

"Drive-your-tractor-to-school day?"

"Yes, every year kids that are old enough to drive a tractor, usually thirteen or so, wash them up and drive 'em to school. It's a big event that they look forward to."

"Noted," I said. "I won't be surprised next time."

The teenager seemed at home in the seat of his massive John Deere. I wondered if his mother made him a hot breakfast every morning. I wondered if she packed his lunch with all his favorites, and if his family shared the details of their day over pot roast and mashed potatoes.

"I want to ride on a tractor, Mom."

I watched a group of teens dismount from their tractors in the parking lot of a Dollar General store a few hundred yards away.

"Mom, can I?"

"I don't see why not."

"Good," she said. "I really want to experience everything here."

I smiled at her use of the word "experience" as we continued our journey to Lisa's house. It was not long before we came to a stop in front of a picture straight from the pages of *Southern Living* magazine. It was a two story, wood framed farmhouse, white, with a wide wraparound front porch. It had wide steps and an old school red front door. The yard was lush and green and filled with large oak trees and azalea bushes; the smells of late spring wafted through the air. The nearest neighbor was at least a half-mile away. It certainly was peaceful, and very quiet compared to the City noise we were used to.

"Did it take you long to adjust to the quiet?"

"I'm still getting used to it," she said thoughtfully, but I then I saw a sadness creep across her face that I didn't recognize. "It's just…Adam, well…you know, he is under so much pressure with the senator." Her voice trailed off as she parked in front of the detached garage. Buddy, the retriever they'd had since he was a pup in New York, emerged sleepily from under the porch and meandered toward us.

"Come on, grab your stuff and I'll show you your room. Z can take a quick nap and we can chat on the porch."

"Mom, I don't need a nap, I'm not a baby," Z protested.

"It's just so you can stay up later tonight," I offered.

"Oh, well, okay then," she conceded and greeted Buddy, grabbed her oversized suitcase and started towards the house, dog in tow.

That is how it is with Zoey. Give her an explanation

that makes sense and she is all in.

Lisa showed us to our room upstairs that was more like a suite than a bedroom. She not only sold high end real estate in SoHo, but she was an accomplished interior designer as well, and her entire home, including our suite, was decorated in what I can only describe as farmhouse chic and there were flowers everywhere, inside and out. It seemed to me that she had adjusted quite well.

I unpacked our clothes and tucked Zoey into a large fluffy bed with overstuffed pillows, where Z discovered a children's book about fishing tucked away under the covers that Lisa left for her.

"Mom, look!" she said excitedly. "Aunt Leese remembered!"

I remembered, too, the lovely conversation Lisa and Zoey had about Z not knowing how to do things in Banjoland, and Lisa's calm reassurance that Zoey would fit in perfectly well. This was a typically thoughtful gesture by Leese.

I met my friend on the porch and plopped down next to her into one of the several large rocking chairs that lined the front of the house.

"I'm so glad you're here, *finally*," she emphasized. She had been "convincing" me for six months to make this move.

"You know, Leese, I feel ready. I really do."

"Good, good. You really need to forget about everything. All of that is behind you now. And you really worry too much. It's all over."

Yes, of course she was right. She was always right. In our lifetime of friendship, dating back to middle school, we were open books with each other, and she was the only one I completely trusted. And that is why I knew, even though her interest in me was genuine, that she was distracted and preoccupied.

"What's wrong?" I asked, sipping on my icy drink.

She hesitated and then sighed, "Something's off. I can't put my finger on it. Ad says it is just pregnancy hormones, but I know that is not it. Something is wrong and I feel like it's something big." She reached across the porch table, taking my hands in hers, like she was reaching for reassurance—which was not like her at all. She was strong and always the voice of logic and reason.

Just then, a large Ford F-250 pick-up truck turned into the driveway, and I immediately smiled as I saw Ad's silhouette behind the wheel. As he got closer I could see the gun rack along the back window, in exactly the same place Lisa had hers, and I chuckled as I thought about these pseudo-Southerners playing their role.

Ad parked and emerged from his truck with the sun creating a contrast that emphasized his frame. He was 6'2" and fit, with broad shoulders and wavy hair brown hair that I noticed he had cut short and that gave him a much more professional appearance than the shag he used to wear. He was also tan, which was unusual for someone who always lectured me on the hazards of being in the sun too much. Lisa's glance and squeeze of my hand told me we would finish our conversation at another time. Adam took the stairs two at a time and dwarfed me with his bear hug. "Lanie, you look great! And where's my little lady?"

As if on cue, Zoey came bounding out of the house, shrugging off nap time, and Adam picked her up and swung her in the air until she giggled herself silly. She begged for more, so he swung her high enough to land atop his shoulders and ran around the yard while she squealed and Buddy nipped at their heels. Thanks to technology and the ability to Facetime, both Lisa and Adam had maintained a strong connection with Zoey (and me) and I was thankful for friends who were closer to us than family.

He jogged to the porch, flipped Zoey over his shoulder, gently set her on the step, and knelt in front of her.

"I've missed you so much," Ad said, "and now that you're here, we are going to have lots of adventures."

Z spontaneously hugged him and took off running into the yard coaxing Buddy to chase her.

"Love that girl," he said as he dragged a rocker towards us. "Missed you too, Lanie," he added with a wink and kissed me on the cheek. He seemed perfectly normal to me.

"Missed you, too. Quite a place you've got here."

"Like it? I think Lisa did an excellent job decorating it, like always. Except for that one time. . ." I interrupted, having repeated this story so often over the years with Ad. It was routine banter between us and Leese, "that time she ordered furniture from overseas for your first apartment and it was so small it was like doll house furniture?"

"And then," Ad said, when she read the descriptions more closely, they said, "'ideal for those under 5 feet tall'?"

"Yeah, yeah," Lisa interjected, "story never gets old. How come you never include that I got a complete refund *and* got to keep the furniture?"

What made this story so funny not only to us, but to those who knew Lisa was that she was immensely talented and a highly sought-after interior designer in New York, and rarely made such a faux pax.

Ad leaned over and kissed her lips softly. "Seriously, how are you feeling?" he asked as he gently put his hand on her belly. "Everything okay? Can I get you anything? That nausea better?"

"I'm good for the moment," she said and plopped her swollen feet into his lap.

"The Jenkins are going to stop over in a few," he offered, rubbing each of her toes methodically and then smiled broadly at me. "Banjoland activities this evening, Lanie."

I smiled at him using our made-up name for Clarksville.

Chapter 2

Ad went in to change and Lisa and I continued to chat on the porch while Zoey flitted about the yard dodging a rambunctious Buddy.

"Do you remember that party I mentioned when we knew what day you would get here?" she asked.

"As I recall," I said, "your exact words were 'wedding in a double wide'.' You were joking, right?"

"Uhm, no. Adam represents constituents from all rungs of society, and it is important for him to be able to relate with everyone."

That made sense to me and if I had to choose someone for that role, it would be Ad.

"If you're tired from travelling, don't feel obligated," she said, "but I am." She sighed. "Normally I like mingling and socializing, but I get tired so easily now, and like I said, something is off with Adam."

I wondered if she was just extra sensitive because of the pregnancy. I was extra sensitive when I was pregnant with Z.

"Just last week he was offered an LC Smith shotgun, you know those are top of the line and hugely expensive," she explained, and continued, "because legislation is coming up he is voting on to change the rules about needing a license to hunt on private land. And that's small potatoes compared to the backdoor thinly veiled quid pro quo's that powerful party backers dangle in front of him all the time."

"We're talking about Ad," I said. "There is nothing to worry about."

I called to Z to come inside so we could get showered and ready for our outing to the doublewide. I wasn't tired and I was eager to see all that life offered here in the deep South, and what better way to start than a wedding in a doublewide.

"Mom, look." She pointed as she skipped towards me. Around the bend in the road and coming quickly towards us was a moving cloud of dust with country music blaring from within. It skidded into the driveway and came to a screeching halt, just inches from Buddy. As the dust lifted, we saw a giant Cyprus tree of a man step out of a battered truck, toss an empty beer can into its bed, and grab another. He wore camo overalls and a hat that said: "Heart of Dixie." His wife, shorter and stout, stepped out of the truck, adjusted herself and tottered over to him.

"Where's the damn Yankee?" he said heartily. It was a bit intimidating.

"I think that's me." I moved closer to say a proper hello. Despite his stereotypical appearance, he seemed friendly enough.

"Well howdy, miss, welcome to God's country. Name's Ray." He grabbed my outstretched hand. "Ray Jenkins. And this here's my ole lady, Mary Sue."

Mrs. Camo smiled shyly, reached out and squeezed my hand with surprising strength.

"Nice to meet you both," I said, shaking Ray's hand as firmly as I could. For some reason I felt like that was important.

"That's my boy, RJ." Ray pointed at a boy around

seven or eight, redundantly dressed in camo shorts and a NASCAR t-shirt, playing with Zoey and Buddy in the front yard.

"So, where's my man?" Ray nodded toward Ad's truck.

"I'll get him," I said and headed towards the house to find Ad.

What politics are bringing these two together? The Jenkins seem friendly enough and despite their stereotypical presentation, are certainly comfortable in their own skin. I think that's why I like them.

I mulled over meeting the Jenkins as I entered the house and climbed the stairs. As I rounded the top, I heard mumbling coming from down the hall. I followed it until I was standing right outside the bedroom door, which was slightly ajar. Adam was on the phone, running his hand through his hair, obviously worried.

"Yes, Senator, I understand," he said softly, but with a tone in his voice that stopped my knock short.

"I don't know how she knows...no, of course not, sir!" Adam said, putting his hand on his forehead and staring blankly out the window with the oddest expression on his face. For a few moments, silence hung heavy. I could feel electricity in the air like just before a thunderstorm. Then lightning struck.

"No, sir. No, sir. I don't know why she's here!" Adam shouted, then glanced around the room to make sure no one had heard him and discovered me, hovering wide-eyed in the doorway, my fist still poised to knock. "Yes, I understand," he said cryptically, immediately regaining his composure. "I'll do my best. Yes, Senator...yes...tonight. I will." He put down the phone and stared at me, eyes stormy, his face contorted and changed. He looked like a man I had never met before. Was he talking about…me?

"What are you doing?" he asked in a suspicious tone I did not recognize. Adam had never said anything even remotely harsh to me before. Who was this person?

"I'm sorry," I said meekly. "I just wanted to tell you Ray was here."

His eyes were angry, cloudy with menace mixed with panic. For a second, I felt afraid of him. Then, the storm passed, and the Adam I knew appeared once more from behind the clouds. I moved instinctively away from him toward the stairs, but he caught me by the arm.

"Lanie, wait," he said. "I'm sorry. Really. I've been under a lot of pressure lately and sometimes it's just a lot to take. I didn't mean to snap at you."

"It's okay, Ad, I understand," I said, although I didn't. Not really.

"Tell Ray I'll be out in a minute, if you don't mind," he said over his shoulder as he stepped into the bathroom and shut the door. He seemed sincere. Maybe I was overreacting, but what if I was the "she" he was talking about. Maybe I had jet lag.

Lisa had followed me into the house and was preparing something to take to the party. I was impressed, because when we were in SoHo and went to a party, we would just stop by the liquor store and show up with whatever was on sale. She was preparing something that looked wild, aged, and poisonous.

"What *is* that?" I asked.

"It's backstrap," she said, with a giggle and a wink. "That's Banjolandese for deer steak. It's a staple in these parts."

I chuckled at her use of "staple in these parts."
Mental Note: backstrap is deer steak.

"Hello friends," Ad announced, coming out onto the porch and glad-handing Ray jovially. It was an odd sight, Adam and Ray together, and I wasn't sure what Adam and Lisa had in common with Ray and Mary Sue, if anything other than a common goal, but I figured all of that would be answered eventually.

"Come help us get ready, Leese," I asked, as she had mentioned that the wedding was Banjoland casual and even though I had no idea what "Banjoland casual" meant, I was certain that nothing in my wardrobe met that description. Lisa rummaged through my clothing options, periodically shaking her head,

"I thought we talked about this," she said, holding up what I thought was a cute vest and tie combo that she repeatedly told me made me look like a flight attendant. "Hold on," she said, and in a few minutes she laid acceptable options on the bed from which I could choose. In record time I tamed my hair into a curly ponytail and whipped together a floral sundress/sandal ensemble. Zoey dressed herself and sporting a blinged out denim ball cap and pink sunglasses, together with Lisa in tow, we descended the staircase slowly and deliberately like a scene from *Gone with the Wind.*

****

The drive, which Ray had said would take about thirty minutes, took us down dirt roads and past old landmarks that radiated history. In the middle of imagining my life on a plantation, I saw our destination come into view. I don't know what I was expecting, but this was surely not it. I was surprised to find our doublewide, complete with faded tin siding, and the obligatory truck up on blocks in the back yard surrounded by crops of some sort.

"Peanuts," Ad said.

"What?"

"Those are peanuts," he explained, "the cash crop here."

"Oh."

We bounced over some potholes in the driveway and parked on the lawn, next to several other vehicles of various makes and models.

"I've never been to a wedding in a trailer before," I said, recollecting out loud.

"Mobile home." Lisa corrected me, smiling.

Mobile home, trailer, tomayto, tomahto, whatever this was it sure had seen its share of sun and wind. The outside was faded with gray patches on the siding, and the place in the middle where the two halves were attached was uneven, as if the ground beneath them had shifted in some great rain two centuries ago. Random pieces of tin around the bottom of the mobile manse served as some type of skirting, which really did not help matters at all. It looked like somebody wearing a skirt with a hem that had come partially undone. An oversized confederate flag flew high above the house. It was the most enormous flag I had ever seen in my life. Periodically a small bulldog would peek out from underneath the screened porch, which was held up by cinder blocks.

"Mom, I want a really cool flag like that for our house, okay?" Zoey asked, as we parked.

"It sure is…big. Maybe one a tad bit smaller, with different colors, okay?"

Despite all the new, the flag was something I would

make a point to address later. The image was everywhere—stickers on vehicle windows, t-shirts, flying from trucks and houses and trail…doublewides. I needed more information so I could understand what it really meant to these people.

"Okay," she said, and I noticed she had pulled her lip gloss out of her purse and was applying it liberally.

"So here's the deal," Lisa said. "This is what you would call a typical shotgun wedding."

"Do people really still use that term?" I asked. "I haven't heard it in years."

"She's three months pregnant and about fifteen years younger than him, I think, but hey, love is ageless."

Ad chuckled and I became more curious about the upcoming nuptials.

As we approached the mobile home/wedding chapel, I was almost knocked over by a dozen half-naked children who tore through the yard, followed by a pack of dogs howling and barking at their heels. They were obviously having the time of their lives.

Adam was immediately embraced by a welcoming committee of about a dozen men, a couple wearing ties, but most in jeans or shorts and holding beers, and who all seemed very happy to see him. He moved through the crowd, shaking hands and slapping backs, hugging ladies and kissing babies like a consummate professional. I felt like I was at a campaign rally. And in this constituency anyway, it appeared he would win any election by a landslide. It appeared the senator had chosen his protégé well. It was part of *the plan*, that Ad was the successor when the senator decided to retire. It was the key to Lisa agreeing to the move.

"Leese," I whispered, but before I could finish,

19

reading my mind like always, she interrupted, "many of these families work in some capacity for the senator or in businesses in which he has ownership, or they want his influence. Sometimes he will stop by an event like this but most of the time he sends Adam as his representative. It endears him to the people that vote. And they vote. Largest turnout in the state."

That made sense, and while we navigated our way through the crowd surrounding Ad, RJ and Z joined the group of children that had gathered around a small pond off to the side of the driveway and across from the mobile home.

"Lanie, this is Billy William and this here is Mrs. Billy William, or as we call her, B," Adam said, putting an arm around each one of them, and pointing at a solitary-looking gentleman smoking nonchalantly beside a rusty burn barrel and a sad looking pink flamingo some yards away. "And that fine gentleman over yonder," he said with a nod and a terrible attempt at a Southern accent, "why that there is Mason." He said it loudly enough for Mason to hear. They acknowledged each other, Mason took a long drag of the cigarette, slipped the lighter into his pocket, and waved.

I smiled and shared pleasantries with Billy William and Mrs. Billy William, but I was distracted by Cigarette Guy. As he approached, my body woke up and took notice. I felt the blood course through my veins. I thought I could hear my heart beating.

God, am I having a stroke? Pull it together Mel, it's not like you have never seen a handsome man before, for God's sake. Not since I met Junior had I experienced such an intense reaction to a man, and it…scared me a little.

"Lanie, Mason…Mason, Lanie," Adam said, making a formal introduction.

Mason took my hand and squeezed it, not too hard, but firmly, confidently, and looked directly into my eyes.

"What's a pretty Yankee doing all the way down in these parts?" he asked with an accent that didn't seem to fit the others and smiled magnificently. His teeth were white and perfect. His eyes were intense, and a vivid emerald green.

"Just checking things out," I said nonchalantly.

I noticed how similar and yet how vastly different he was from everyone else at the wedding. He was wearing Cole Haan casual shoes. All the other men were wearing flip-flops or boots of some sort. He certainly was an outlier in this group. His shorts were khaki, not camo, with ironed creases, and they hugged his body in all the right places. His shirt was a sea foam green, collared polo that highlighted his eyes, with two buttons undone. It framed his fit torso and revealed powerful but fluid biceps. He was tan and statuesque, and I inherently wondered what was wrong with him. Despite his hunky good looks, my marriage to Junior taught me to be wary of the cover and to read a few chapters of the book before purchasing it. Besides, becoming involved with a man was on the bottom of my to do list—no offense to him personally.

Lisa leaned in and whispered into my ear, "Like what you see?" and she snorted in the silly way that she did when she was picking at me. I vaguely remember a late-night conversation about a guy she thought I might find "interesting," which is a word she always used when she meant hot.

"Is this that guy? What's not to like? But I told you

before, I'm not looking for a relationship."

She just scoffed in the way she always did when she thought I was being ridiculous.

"What are you doing here, man?" Adam questioned as he reached out to shake Mason's hand. It sounded almost like an accusation.

"The bride's mother works at the Club," said Mason. "You know," he continued, "the country club. She has been Mother's personal favorite for years. She asked that I drop off a contribution on her behalf to the happy couple," he explained and winked at me as the happy couple swept past us, hollering at each other at the top of their lungs that it was time to get the wedding started.

Odd, all the hollering, but no one seemed to react—like it was normal behavior.

Mase's explanation seemed to put Adam at ease, and his body relaxed. Mason had achieved his intended result. He had handled Adam expertly—but why would Ad be suspicious?

"What about you, man? What brings you to this catered affair?" Mason continued pleasantly.

"Ah, you know, business as usual," Ad said.

"Since when is a wedding in a trailer business as usual for you?" Mason quizzed.

"Mobile home," I corrected him with a grin.

"Standing in for the senator, you know how it goes. These folks are friends of ours."

The conversation between them appeared friendly enough on the surface, but there was obviously, at least to me, some underlying tension between these two.

"We should probably head inside and take our seats, or we won't be able to see the show…I mean, wedding,"

Ad said, lighter now, as he held up his fingers to make air quotes around the word "wedding," and we walked towards the trailer/mobile home. Just then RJ and a smaller, dark-haired boy with piercing blue eyes, no shirt, and a jagged scar above his belly button bolted across the yard toward us, out of breath.

"Miss Lanie, y'all come with us, hurry, we got somethin' to show ya," RJ said, smiling and running behind the other boy, motioning for us to follow. Zoey took off behind them, trying her best to keep up, until they abruptly stopped next to an old chicken coop that served as a border between the yard and the woods. We changed course, making small talk, towards the pen.

"Hang on a sec," the boy said, holding out his hand at us like a traffic cop, while he and RJ slipped into the open door of the old coop.

They reappeared a minute later.

"Look what we found!" they yelled in unison.

I screamed and stumbled backwards. Mason moved quickly to catch me just as I was about to hit the ground. My cheeks were burning, and I felt a bit flush. His strong arms were around my waist and his body towered over mine as he scooped me up and righted me, and the smell of his musky cologne distracted me as I tried to regain my balance. I knew any chance to make a good first impression on these people had just evaporated.

"Need to expect the unexpected in this part of the Country," Mase offered, kindly ignoring the spectacle I had just created. Zoey was oblivious as she kept her eyes focused on the scene in front of her.

"Thanks," I said sheepishly, straightening my sundress and playing it off.

Lisa shrugged like me making a spectacle of myself

was a normal occurrence—

typical behavior for me.

Mason smiled in a way that resonated with me as genuine and offered a simple "anytime."

I oriented myself towards RJ and Blues Eyes, and at first, I didn't think it was real

but when it took a step toward us, I had no doubt whatsoever. In front of the smelly coop and between an old rusty barrel filled with crushed beer cans and a few buckets of corn, Blue Eyes had a baby alligator...on a leash! It was about two feet long and it was wagging its tail because it was swishing back and forth...It just stared at us, swishing its tail in its camo collar and leash.

I must be in the Twilight Zone.

"I didn't mean to scare you ma'am," Blue Eyes said earnestly, "he won't hurt nobody. Dan's been with us since he was hatched." He was sweet and sincere in his effort to convince me Dan was harmless, but there was so much information in that one sentence. He called me "ma'am" which made me feel old and respected at the same time, the alligator had a name and he's a pet. As I was processing this information a man wearing a "Baby Daddy" t-shirt suddenly materialized alongside of me. "What's the big deal? That's just Dan," he said. "He won't hurt nobody. He's family." He took the leash from Blue Eyes and motioned for me to come closer. Instinctively I reached for Mason's arm.

"The alligator's name is Dan?" I asked as I grabbed Z's outstretched hand and we slowly approached the beast.

"Well, technically, it's Lieutenant Dan, see...he's missing part of his back leg," Blue Eyes said, lifting him up so I could see, and referring to the movie *Forest*

Gump. I busted out laughing at this reference and that an alligator would be someone's family pet—a pet they were quite proud to have.

"Can I pet him, Mom? Please?"

In a million years I would never have expected the need to answer a question like this from Z, and that's when I knew it was going to take some time to learn the rules of our new home.

Dan's introduction was interrupted by a grandmotherly woman in the doorway shouting so loudly that even Lieutenant Dan almost jumped out of his skin.

"Y'all come on inside now! Let's get this show on the road!"

Mason and I, along with the rest of our group, headed towards the wedding chapel/mobile home and fell in line behind Baby Daddy and Red Solo Cup girl. Lisa and Adam were directly behind us, followed by what sounded like a gaggle of cackling geese, about thirty or forty people in all, I guessed.

"Get ready for your first, how should I describe it? Uhm…non-traditional wedding," Mason said with that sexy grin. He was flirty and I was unexpectedly interested.

"I'm ready," I said. I was ready to see this how this entire production unveiled itself.

We walked past two beer kegs that looked like gargoyles on each side of a worn path and followed the line up some rickety steps through the side door into the main room of the doublewide, which was strewn with crepe paper and balloons. Once inside, Mason dropped an unmarked envelope into a box strategically placed at the beginning of a make-shift aisle.

25

We took our seats next to Lisa and Ad and made small talk while we waited for the ceremony to begin. The children remained outside under the supervision of a kind looking girl of around sixteen who at my last check was herding them into a game of hide and seek.

"So, what do you here in Clarksville?" I asked.

"Government work, nothing too exciting. In a nutshell, my parents practically founded the town, I went to boarding school with plans to work in Washington, DC, plans changed and here I am."

The way he looked at me when he spoke made me feel like he could see through me. I felt exposed and so I turned away.

Our conversation was interrupted when someone hit play on a boom box (people still use these?), and the ceremony began. Out of my periphery I noticed an older man with a gray goatee and slicked-back gray hair taking a swig out of a Jack Daniels bottle he had in his back pocket. I watched him stumble drunkenly up the aisle expecting him to take a seat with the rest of us, but instead he took his place at the front of the crowd. When he got there, I swear he hiccupped.

"Who is that?"

"That? Why that is the Reverend Hokum," said Mason. "He's the minister round these parts. Funerals are twenty bucks, weddings are thirty—plus all the free Jack Daniels he can drink. Not a bad bargain as long as you don't mind if he gets the names wrong."

"Are you serious?" I'd never heard of such a thing.

Mason nodded. He was amusing without being judgmental, and I smiled at this quality. It was as if he understood and somehow had come to love and appreciate this crazy world, even though he clearly was not a part of it in the way everyone else seemed to be.

When the bride appeared, pausing briefly to savor her moment in the limelight, she appeared desperately young, and in some peculiar way ethereal and strangely beautiful despite the fact that she was wearing a tube top. As she made her way solemnly down the aisle to meet her fate, I felt a vague sadness that I couldn't quite explain. I found myself wondering what her life would be like after the wedding was over. What kind of a future could she ever expect to have? Would she be happy, or would she be trapped in a miserable life with a man who wasn't what he appeared to be? I felt a bit of kinship with her in that moment.

"Dearly Beloved, we are gathered here today," said the Reverend Hokum, who then hiccupped and lost his place, so he took it again from the top. "Dearly Beloved, we are gathered here today to witness the marriage of Sarah Jane and…" Then he tried again.

"Everyone, glad y'all are here to witness the marriage of Sarah Jane and . . ." He stared at the groom.

"Told you he wouldn't get the name," Mason whispered.

We both had to exercise some serious self-control to keep from laughing out loud. Finally, the reverend managed to croak out something that might vaguely have resembled the groom's name, and the rings and vows were hurriedly exchanged, and Miss Sarah Jane became Mrs. Signed, Sealed, and Delivered.

Afterwards, Mason invited me to have a drink at his truck, which seemed to be the common drinking venue at this event, where he offered "different options" than a keg full of Busch Lite. My skin tingled as he stood next to me and let down his tailgate. In front of us was a large wooden box with hinges and a lock. In less than a minute, before us was a make-shift bar. Not only did it have glasses, it had wine, various liquors and mixers, and in the center a covered ice container. I was impressed and apprehensive at the same time. Either this was a sign that he was prepared for any occasion, or he was a player prepared to impress his next conquest. I shook off my doubt and accepted a vodka tonic, my drink of choice when socializing.

"Welcome to Banjoland," he said, tapping his Corona gently against my glass.

"Cheers," we said in unison.

"So Lanie, I'd love to show you around the County whenever you have some free time. Bring Zoey, too."

He was easy to be with and I felt an underlying draw to him that was unlike any chemistry I'd felt before. It was more like an energy

"I'd love that," I said and smiled, ignoring some initial hesitation and deciding there was no harm in hanging out and learning about my new home.

Our moment was disrupted when we heard a car door slam and voices arguing in the distance.

"What was that?" I asked.

"I'm not sure," he answered, as we searched for the source of the noise.

Then I noticed at the end of the tree line, past several camo trucks, a black Cadillac. It was about 50 yards away hard to see because it was dusk, and the car blended in with the dark spaces between the trees.

"Look," I said, and pointed towards the car. The front driver's side door of the Caddy was cracked open. I could not see the driver clearly, but I did see a slightly sinister-seeming guy in sunglasses hand Adam an envelope, which Adam hastily folded and put in his front pocket.

"I thought Ad was here to make a contribution, not receive one," I said out loud without thinking. Mason nodded like he was thinking the same thing.

Ad turned to walk away while sinister-sunglasses guy was still talking, and Sunglasses didn't seem happy about it. He unexpectedly reached out and shoved Adam.

"Tell him not to spend it all in one place!" Sunglasses yelled. Adam swung around to face him and said something back that we could not hear when the driver's side door of the sedan opened completely. I assumed the driver was going to get out and put an end to this escalating scuffle. Adam immediately pushed him back inside the car, almost closing it on him, but just before he disappeared once more behind tinted windows he turned towards me and our eyes briefly met before the Caddy disappeared down the tree line.

My body shivered. I began to tremble, and my heart started beating so fast and so loudly I thought it was audible.

"Are you okay? Is something wrong?" Mase quizzed, sensing my obvious distress despite my attempt to hide it. I convinced myself it must be the jet lag combined with alcohol that had caused my imagination to work overtime. It was impossible.

"Nothing," I said, downplaying my overreaction. "It's just…that guy in the car reminded me of someone I used to know."

"Well judging by the look on your face, "used to know" is a good thing. Do you want to talk about it?"

I most definitely did not want to talk about it.

"Let's just go join the party," I suggested,

intentionally upbeat, and so we left the make-shift tailgate bar, but I couldn't shake the vision of the man in the Caddy.

Chapter 3

Morning sounds were different in Banjoland, the birds especially. They were exceedingly verbal announcing the dawn of a new day. I had been an early riser since well before Zoey was born, relishing the start of a new day with new possibilities. I crept quietly down the stairs, poured myself a cup of coffee that Lisa had ordered especially for me from our favorite New York coffee shoppe, and headed outside to the porch so I could enjoy the solitude and replay the events from the previous evening at the trailer/mobile home.

"Nice bed head," Lisa said. Her voice startled me and I almost spilled my coffee.

I ignored her comment about my regular morning look. "What are you doing up so early?"

"Couldn't sleep, baby moves whenever he wants, without much concern for me, and I knew you'd be up so here I am." She seemed so young and almost fragile as the morning sun streaked through trees and landed on her face.

"That was quite a wedding." She chuckled and took a long sip of her coffee.

I smiled and nodded as I recalled my introduction to Lieutenant Dan. "There were so many firsts for me."

"So what did you think?" she asked, and I knew what she meant.

"About what?" I asked, making her say it.

"Mason, duh."

"He's nice," I said, skimming over the intent of her question. I had something else on my mind. She rolled her eyes and shook her head. "But there is something else."

Lisa leaned in like she was about to receive a national security secret and it reminded me of our weekend morning gossip sessions from when we lived in SoHo. "Do tell," she said eagerly.

"I think I saw Junior." It sounded ridiculous as soon as the words slipped past my lips.

Her response was immediate. "What do you mean you think you saw Junior? We were all there that night. We all saw what happened."

That was true. We were all there, Lisa, Ad, and me. And we all saw it with our own eyes.

"I know it sounds crazy," I said, and explained the tree line Cadillac encounter, Sunglasses, Ad and the Junior clone.

"Weird," she said, "all of it. But we both know it's impossible. And don't you think," she added thoughtfully, "that if somehow Junior *was* alive and Adam knew he would say something?"

"Of course," I said, feeling immediately reassured, "I hadn't even thought of that." It was probably the jetlag.

Chapter 4

"Are you ready?" Mason asked, producing a single daisy and sporting his sexy smile on the other side of the screen door.

"I am." I fiddled with my hair—straightened for the occasion and tied into a neat ponytail with a piece of camo ribbon (when in Rome), which made me laugh at myself but nevertheless thought was a nice touch.

"Where are we going?"

"You'll see. Where's Zoey?"

"She declined and literally said 'I don't want to cramp your style mom', so she is with Lisa getting their nails done."

He chuckled and smiled as we drove for a while on country back roads making small talk until we reached an open hayfield next to an old wooden farmhouse. He parked next to the house and came around to open my door. I liked that he had manners.

He produced two ball caps for us. His read, "The 2nd amendment. Period."

Mine said, "Bullet Bob's Discount Ammo," just like the hat Leese was wearing when we arrived but before we became official residents.

"What is this place?" I asked. It was picturesque. Really beautiful...no concrete anywhere. I was completely content to be outside on a sunny afternoon and the more I engaged with Mason the more I relaxed and enjoyed myself.

"It is part of our family farm," he said, and plundered through the toolbox in the back of the truck, handing me a shotgun, and put a box of shells, along with a larger closed box, on the tailgate. "We're going to shoot skeet."

I had zero experience with guns, and I didn't know anyone who owned one (sans Leese and Ad, and that was new). I also had no idea what a skeet was. The look on my face must have tipped him off.

"Trust me, you'll enjoy yourself as soon as you feel the power you hold in your hands."

"Hmm, if you say so," I said, uncertain about how I felt about shooting a defenseless skeet.

I was even more puzzled when he opened the larger box filled with round, brightly colored orange disks, and I made the mistake of admitting that I thought a skeet was an animal. He tried to contain his laughter as he loaded the clay discs into the thrower, a plastic device with a horseshoe-type opening at the end where the skeet was placed.

Before he could school me on the shooting process, the *Mission Impossible* theme song arose from his back pocket. He reached for his phone, glanced at it and gently set his gun down on the tailgate.

"Excuse me just a for a minute," he said. "I need to take this."

He answered the phone and took a few steps toward the front of the truck, but I could still hear his side of the conversation.

"Yes?" he said. "I know. It's about to hit the fan. We just need a few more nails for the coffin." His voice was edgy and harsh. "I told you to leave it to me," he added, and hung up.

That was ominous, I thought. And his tone was serious. I wondered what he meant by "nails for the coffin?"

"Now where were we?" he said, retracing his steps as he settled on the tailgate, changing his tone completely and flashing that grin. He put the phone back in his pocket and didn't mention the call.

We sat on the tailgate while he unpacked earplugs and a small cleaning kit. I inhaled his musky smell as he taught me the ins and outs of gun safety, and my heart began to wake.

"So, Mase, what exactly do you do for the government?" I asked, the phone call helping me realize that I didn't know many details about his life.

"Well," he said, stacking the skeet in a neat and orderly row next to us, "I'm a special agent. I focus on government corruption, racketeering and the like. I love it."

Banjoland's very own Deep Throat. Except that he exposed government officials. It sounded dangerous.

But then came the bombshell.

"My father wanted to groom me for a life of politics," he continued, loading a skeet, "but I knew that wasn't for me. Said I had the looks and people skills to go far, but I just didn't like the quid pro quo. It seemed too sleazy for me—not that I am a choir boy by any means," he added, "I just like to do things the right way."

He handed me a beer.

"So instead of me, he has Adam."

After quickly making the connection, I sought confirmation.

"You're Senator Downes' son?"

35

Why hadn't anyone told me this?

"Yes, my lady, I am Mason Westhoven Downes IV." He bowed in an exaggerated manner and kissed my hand like we were English royalty.

I was intrigued as my mind began filling in blanks. I wondered if he knew anything about what was going on with Adam...and could this explain the tension that was palpable between them at the shotgun wedding.

Chapter 5

My job interview was in an insane asylum. The only reason I know this is because as I walked along the sidewalk toward the entrance of the ivy-covered, two-story building that looked like it belonged on a college campus, I noticed a large corner foundational block that said "Clarksville Asylum, built 1906" peeking through the leafy vines. It instantly reminded me of that frigid winter day not too long after my baby sister Sissy died. I thought I had erased it from my memory.

****

On that day snowflakes the size of silver dollars were falling so thickly that we could barely see. I remember thinking how odd it was at first to visit her here. My father circled the block, navigating the homeless and drunks, trying to find a place to park as close as he could.

Finally, he found a vacant spot on the third floor of a parking ramp catty corner from the entrance. Surprisingly, he parked between the lines.

"Remember what I said," he told me, his stale alcohol breath permeating the air.

I learned not to acknowledge that.

"I know," I said, eager to get away from him.

I hated him. I hated him for Sissy, and I hated him for my mom.

It was dark and visiting hours were almost over as I

hurried down the sidewalk, he meandering behind, past the street people asking for spare change, past the waiting cabs and the overwhelming smell of exhaust, until it was directly in front of me. Some days…summer days…when the trees were green and the sun was shining, it was welcoming. But in the winter, through the barren trees, shadows fell in disturbing shapes and forms—the vines climbing, searching, from one window to the next…winter was much different at Bellevue.

My father caught up to me, took a swill from the paper bag he negotiated from one of the street people, and we, what was left of our family, walked up the steps together. I still had hope that one day she would come home. With Sissy the loss was sudden, a car accident at the hands of our drunk father, and as traumatic as it was to have my seven-year-old sister ripped from our lives, this was in some ways worse. It was the hope. There was always hope, they said, that she might get better, and so with every visit, no matter how hard I tried, I could not distinguish that smoldering ember of hope. But this visit was different

"And so," he said, in his sterile white coat glancing up from her medical chart, "do either of you have any questions?"

My father took a swig from his bag.

"Yes," I choked out, "are you sure?" I felt stupid as soon as I asked, I mean he was the doctor.

"I'm afraid so," he answered politely.

I wondered how many other "loved ones" got similar news today.

"Your mother has been in this psychotic state since Sissy died over 10 years ago. The likelihood of her recovering is miniscule."

Miniscule.

My heart ached and I was overwhelmed with deep sadness while I tried to make sense of why today was the day they chose for my mother to die.

****

The front doors of the Clarksville Asylum still had bars across them from back in the day, and the first thing I noticed was how it was unlike Bellevue. Well, except for the bars. It was clean and modern, and the lobby wasn't filled with the homeless and patients in strait jackets randomly yelling obscenities without purpose. There was one person, a very tall, neatly dressed, Native American man seated in the corner near the television, watching intently. Once he noticed me, he stood up, brushed off his ironed slacks and shirt, and reached out his hand toward mine. His hair was shoulder length, jet black and shiny, and he wore it loose. He appeared to be fiftyish and was quite handsome.

"Welcome," he said in a firm bass voice that reminded me of Johnny Cash, "my name is Patamon, but folks call me Pat."

"Thanks," I said. "I'm Lanie and I have an interview at ten."

"One minute," he said. "Have a seat and I'll let them know you're here."

He was pleasant and I hoped the job would work out because I would really enjoy telling people I worked in the nut house.

While I waited for my interview to begin, I replayed the events of my inaugural Banjoland week in my mind and tried to fit together a few pieces of this puzzle. Even though I had no facts, it was obvious that something weird was going on with Adam. A cursory review of the information has him acting strangely short tempered, meeting a guy in sunglasses along a wood line at night and receiving an envelope, plus an odd interaction with Mason. I still had a lingering apprehension about the man in the Cadillac, but I took reassurance from the fact that Ad was there, and I trusted him almost as much as I trusted Lisa. Lisa didn't have much more information to add, except that she knew something was going on that involved the Native Americans from the reservation, because Ad mentioned something about casinos and revenue.

If I learned anything during my relationship with Junior, it was to trust that inner voice I once habitually ignored, and so I silently appreciated that for a minute while I waited for Mr. Peel.

The interview was a breeze. My experience working for non-profits and fundraising fit nicely into the management of a large umbrella organization that oversaw the County's human services programs.

"That's all I have," said Mr. Peel. "Do you have any questions?"

I had a few, but overall the vibe was good, the money was okay, but the icing on the cake was I really did want to tell people I worked in an asylum.

He offered me the job, welcomed me to town, and invited me and Z to dinner once we were "fully settled in."

****

"Well?" Lisa asked as soon I walked through the door.

Her belly was getting bigger by the day. It wouldn't be long until Adam Junior, AJ as we had been calling him, would arrive.

"Well, what?" I said, milking the moment.

"You know, how'd it go?" she asked.

Zoey piped up. "Hey, Mom, Aunt Lisa said now that we moved here, I can help her pull the weeds from her garden."

"Wow, how nice of her," I said. "But Aunt Lisa has Uncle Adam for that. You're going to be *my* weed puller. Anyway, I got the job."

"I knew you would!"

She and Zoey danced around to the song "Way Down Yonder on the Chattahoochee," which was playing on the radio, and for some reason we started talking about growing okra.

Next up was to find a place for me and Z to live. And a place to shop, get coffee and get our nails/hair done. I probably didn't need to worry too much about that since Lisa was much more high maintenance than me, and Zoey was in her pre-maintenance stage.

"What's up?" Ad asked, walking in in mid-celebration,

"My mom got the job!" She took his hand and pulled him around the kitchen to join in the dance.

"Really? Interesting," he said, "so I guess you really are here for good."

"Seems that way," I said.

"Well, that's great, Lanie, just great." He went to the fridge, popped open a beer and drank it all in one swallow. Then he drank another one.

Chapter 6

It hadn't taken long to get physically settled into our small, two-bedroom country house, halfway between Lisa's and the asylum. She said I should probably stop calling it the asylum—that Zoey would start calling it that, too—and then everyone else would call it that and then we'd have another Dick's Buttkiss situation on our hands (circa ninth grade). She was probably right.

****

From the summer before seventh grade when I met her, Lisa had been my best friend. Without her, I'm not sure I would've been able to deal with loving Junior…how he died…or my dismal family, but what really cemented our friendship was the kindness she showed me on the worst day of my life.

On that rainy gray winter day, as we stood in the entryway of St Mary's Catholic Church on Grand Street preparing to bury my seven-year-old sister, the one joy in my life and who was killed riding in a car with my father while he was drunk, Lisa was my rock. Her funeral was a poor charade. My parents performed their obligatory roles, receiving condolences and playing their part, but I was furious. I was furious that his drunkenness hadn't already done enough damage to our family, but that now it took away the one bright spot we had, and I was furious at my mother for staying with him and subjecting all of us to his drunken rage. Now Sissy was gone and I was engulfed by terrible sadness. Nothing made sense and nothing was reliable, except for Lisa, who held me while I sobbed. And she has been solid for me since that day.

****

"Hey sexy lady."

My body reacted to the sound of his voice.

"Hey."

My lips were chapped from kissing him so much.

We had been dating a little over a month, since the skeet shoot/date, and every visit, text and phone call made me want another. I had never met a special agent, and his combination of law enforcement, good looks and genuine kindness was a potent intoxicant and I was falling for him, telling myself along the way to be cautious, but finding that more and more difficult. My only long-term relationship had been with Junior, and it started out the same way, filled with excitement and chemistry.

I married Junior—his real name was John Robert, and most called him J.R., but I affectionately called him Junior—when I was eighteen after dating since we were fifteen. I saw him as an escape from the hell I lived in at home, and he treated me better than I had been treated by anyone. I loved him deeply. We were not married long before his behavior towards me changed. He became harsh and demanding and in an outburst of anger he would occasionally slap me or shove me—but he always had an apology and a warning that I shouldn't make him angry. The anger escalated into unpredictable bouts of more physical rage, but by then we'd had Zoey and he threatened to take her from me whenever I mentioned leaving him. I was young and scared and wondered if it was all somehow my fault, so I stayed. If it weren't for Ad and Lisa, I probably wouldn't have made it. And now it feels similar, but different at the same time.

Because Mase was going to be out of town for a few days, I knew tonight was going to be "the" night. He had patiently waited without pressuring me and I was nervous, eager, apprehensive—a smorgasbord of emotions and I wanted to offer the best. I spent more time than I'd like to admit getting my nails done, shaving every visible hair on my body, and all the womanly things women do before they sleep with a man for the first time. After trying on almost everything I own, I finally settled on a pair of torn jean shorts and a cute "Bullet Bob's" t-shirt.

"You look great," he said, dropping his twelve-pack onto the floor and pulling me tightly up against him. He kissed me softly at first, but then it was urgent.

Our bodies were alive and connected.

Before I could put his beer in the fridge, he picked me up and straddled my legs around his waist.

He carried me down the hall, knocked over a picture on a side table with my foot, stumbled into my room and in one motion we were on my bed with our lips still locked. He slid his knee between my legs and spread them apart so he could position himself directly on top of me. He began a slow grind. We undressed in record time, tossing our clothes anywhere, and I wrapped my legs around his to hold him firmly in place as he started to enter me, when unexpectedly, I began to cry. I tried to stop but it seemed the more I tried, the more I cried. Mase must have felt the tears on my cheek because he pulled back, surprised.

"What's wrong, am I hurting you?" he asked gently.

I don't know! I don't know what's wrong with me!

I could feel my face turning read and it felt like I was having hot flashes.

"No, no," I mumbled, "nothing is wrong, really. I'm so sorry, I don't know why I'm crying."

I turned away from him, mortified, and wiped my tears on my new pillow sham.

I had kept my emotions under wraps for so long that they just came bubbling out uncontrollably. I hadn't been with a man that I cared about since Junior all those years ago and that wasn't a conscious choice, just a routine way of life.

"I'm okay, really. I am."

I am a complete basket case.

He slid off to the side of me, propped himself up on his elbow and gently turned my face toward him. I couldn't meet his eyes. He stroked my cheek with the back of his hand.

"It's okay," he said softly.

My feelings were unguarded and raw, and his kindness began the crumble of the emotional wall I had built long ago.

I leaned up and tenderly kissed the base of his neck and worked my way to his waiting lips. I wanted to feel close to him. Our bodies moved together symbiotically, first slowly, his body like a wave repetitively crashing into mine until he tensed, and we shared that intimate closeness I hoped wouldn't end.

****

I arranged for Z to spend Saturday with RJ, as they had developed a mentor/mentee type of relationship. RJ felt that it was his responsibility to school Zoey in the

Banjoland ways, and I have to say, for a seven-year-old, he seemed to have them down pretty well. In the short time we'd been here, he taught her how to tell poisonous snakes from the friendly ones—pointy heads and red touching black means stay back. Round heads and black touching yellow—means he is a good fellow. He also taught her how to track deer and how to find their scrapes on the ground and on the trees. Lisa assured me she would be okay in their (our) world, so I encouraged her to pay attention so she could teach me everything she learned.

I left early Saturday morning for Lisa's and dropped Zoey at Ray and Mary Sue's, along with a change of clothes because, as Mary Sue reminded me, "it's awful hot mid-day. Kids'll probably need to cool off some."

"Remember your sunscreen, Z, and to keep your t-shirt on, even when you're in the water."

She sighed. "I've been a ginger all my life, Mom. I know the drill."

"She's a bit sassy today," Mary Sue observed. She took the towel and sunscreen from me.

I chuckled. "Wonder where she gets that from?"

"I wonder." She smiled kindly.

RJ waved for Zoey to join him in their version of a swimming pool.

Ray had stacked up bales of hay in a circle in their back yard, probably twenty-five feet in diameter and about four feet high, thrown a tarp over the entire circle and secured it around the hay with ratchet straps. Then he filled the center of the circle with water from a garden hose, and voila, a swimming pool. According to Ad, it was an annual creation that lasted until the first weekend in October, when dove-shooting season opened—the official indicator of the change of seasons.

After a quick kiss and hug, she flew across the grass, climbed a hay bale and cannon balled her way into the day.

As I pulled into Lisa's driveway, Adam stepped off the porch toward his truck. I thought he would already be gone. His moods, according to Leese, were still unpredictable, but now that we were semi-settled, I could have a legitimate, private conversation with her and try to figure out what was going on, because it was obvious something was happening.

"Hey, Lanie Lou." He walked by me and opened his truck door, dumped in his briefcase and snack bag, and turned to face me for a minute. "How're you enjoying the nut house?" he asked as he climbed into his truck.

"You know," I joked, "I'm the only one not on medication, so there's that."

He chuckled, gave me a wave—and he was off. He seemed perfectly normal.

I carried the still warm box of Krispy Kreme donuts that she had asked, well, begged for, that wafted of sugar and had Buddy glued to my feet. The morning was my favorite part of the day. It was cool and the humidity hadn't yet settled on us like a smothering wool blanket.

Lisa met me on her front porch, holding two cups of coffee—one with whipped cream, obviously mine. This was one of the things I really liked about the South. Front porches. Every house had one, and when it was cool, well cooler, it was the perfect vantage point to observe everything, nothing, or in our world—just to read the latest *Cosmo*.

"Hi, friend," I said, as Leese ambled toward the small wicker table, slid out a chair from underneath it with one of her pregnancy related swollen feet, and slowly lowered herself onto the cushion without spilling a drop of our coffee. It still surprised me how good she looked this far along in her pregnancy, the twenty extra pounds notwithstanding.

Buddy plopped down under the table, familiar with the ritual that we would covertly slip him a bite of whatever we were eating in order to avoid the predictable lecture from Adam that "dogs don't need to eat table food."

"Hey, Mel." She took a sip with one hand, snapping her fingers and pointing toward the donuts with the other.

"Calm down." I slid the box toward her.

Without any hesitation, she literally tore open the box and began devouring each soft sugar delight one by one, sometimes taking a momentary break to dunk it in her coffee.

"Geez, Leese, take some time to breathe," I said, noting the irony of the fitness queen herself shoveling donuts into her face. I was half tempted to record it on my phone for amusement later but decided against it for the sake of our friendship. Midway through the fourth donut she began to relax and breathe easily.

"You act like you haven't eaten in a week," I joked, wiping the smidge of whipped cream I could feel on my upper lip.

"You don't understand," she said as she continued to chew, "it's been an extra-stressful few days."

She swallowed, took another sip of coffee and then a deep breath. She exhaled slowly. "You know why we moved here," she said, "it was supposed to be a stepping-stone for Adam's political career, and Senator Downes agreed to take him on as a protégé as a favor to my dad and get him on the fast track."

I knew all about the plan. Lisa's dad was a senator and was in the same college fraternity with Senator Downes.

She continued, "Well, it hasn't exactly been what we thought it would be."

She fumbled with the last donut, tore it into small pieces, and fed them one by one to Buddy, who was drooling all over her feet.

I reached across the table and took her hand in mine and squeezed it gently. Her eyes started to water a little and I could tell she was doing her best to hold back the tears.

"What is it?" I whispered.

"Oh, Mel," she blurted. Tears began to flow. "I'm so confused."

I nodded, encouraging her to continue.

"You know about the damn plan," she said, "but Adam's changed. Something's going on and he won't tell me what it is."

"How do you mean he's changed?" I asked, knowing what I had seen but wondering if there was more.

"His mood is so unpredictable. One minute he is normal, the next he gets a call, and he is off the deep end. Whenever I ask him what is going on, he just says 'business.' I get it. I get that I am not supposed to know everything and that I should to accept what he says and let it go. But when did we start acting like he was the Godfather and I'm not supposed to ask him about his business? Maybe I am just overreacting with all the hormones and everything, but Mel, I know something big is happening. I can feel it."

I looked at her sweet face, covered in worry and sugar from the donuts crusting around her lips. I had to smile.

"What?" she said.

"You have donut crust around your mouth." I reached across the table with a napkin to wipe it off. "And here's the deal. If Ad won't tell you what's going on, then we'll do what we always do when we want to find out something. We'll figure it out for ourselves."

Chapter 7

I was glad we decided to team up, Leese and me, because if something was shady with Ad and the senator, me spending time with Mason and she with Ad would increase our odds of finding out what it was. And besides, the fact that we were best friends just meant that we were supposed to figure this out together, in our minds anyway. Her behavior that morning on her porch had been so out of character. I wondered myself how much of her feelings were due to hormones and stress.

Adam and the senator were at the statehouse in Tallahassee because they were introducing some "important legislation that could change our future," Ad had mysteriously informed us, refusing to give details. He did seem a bit more optimistic and a tad less cranky lately. Lisa was about ready to have their baby, whose due date was a few weeks away.

****

We'd been as careful as we could to avoid being seen but since it was Friday afternoon, I wasn't all that worried. The fact that businesses shut down on Fridays at noon in the South was still a new concept to me, but it served us well today. We parked behind the Dairy Queen, proceeded with determination through the maze of tree roots and fallen branches that was the backyard of Miss Myrna's Pies & Cakes, and inched along the side of the neighboring printing company. Ad's office was inside a beautiful antebellum home just off Main Street, about a block from the courthouse. The town was deserted save for a random visitor to the gas station preparing to head out for the weekend. From what Ad had told us, the office used to have slave quarters upstairs and slaves were only allowed to use the back staircase to get to it.

"Not many people even today know it's there," he had said, referring to the back staircase. And then as if he had caught himself, added, "Not like it's a big secret or anything. We just don't advertise it."

We entered the house through the back door as quickly as we could once we figured out which key Lisa scarfed from Adam's "extra key" bowl on the kitchen counter was the right one and took a minute to orient ourselves before putting our plan in motion.

"This way." Lisa led us through the kitchen, past the imported coffee and various gourmet food packages prominently displayed on the pristine granite countertop, to what I thought was the pantry. She opened the door and stepped inside. I followed her. It was, in fact, a large pantry, and its shelves were filled with boxes of bourbon, whiskey, vodka—you name it. They were prepared for any celebratory occasion. Lisa slowly pulled the shelves forward. They were braced against a wall that also served as a hidden door and led to the back staircase. It was narrow but heavy, and the many cobwebs covering the hinges suggested it had not been used in quite some time. I wasn't sure why we were even using these stairs since no one was in the office, but Lisa insisted we do everything we could to avoid being seen.

"What if the cleaning staff shows up? What if someone sees us through a window?"

I didn't argue with her.

We crept up the secret back staircase toward Adam's second floor office as stealthily as we could, climbing the narrow steps slowly to compensate for Lisa's extra twenty pounds, until we reached the top and gently pushed open the smaller than normal, dated wooden door.

It was a comfortable space, albeit a man space. The office itself had a soft leather couch, two matching chairs and a credenza under the window—which had a lovely view of the monster oak trees on the lawn.

"What exactly are we looking for?" asked Leese, continuing to sneak around the office.

"Let's just see what we can find, but remember to leave everything the same as it was," I cautioned…as if somehow I was an experienced sleuth. "I'll start with this side of the desk, and . . ."

The faint sound of a door clicking shut interrupted my instructions, and panic struck as we stood still and waited with anticipation to see if we heard was actually the door shutting. In a few seconds I heard footsteps on the creaky stairs. I grabbed Lisa's hand and pulled her as fast as I could across the room to the back staircase, my heart beating through my chest—my mind racing with plausible explanations of why we were there. I was moving at breakneck speed. In the process of pulling her through the door she almost fell down the stairs. Thankfully, she grabbed onto the railing and stopped the impending disaster in an acrobatic form I had never seen before without uttering a sound. I fumbled with the door handle, trying to secure it shut, but it was so old and warped it would not close tightly.

We froze.

I heard a key turn in the lock and then the door to the office slowly opened. There was silence for a moment. I heard the door click shut and then silence again.

I peered through the slit in the door and gasped so loudly I was sure I'd been heard. Leese put her hand over my mouth and pushed my shoulder aside so she could see what I saw through the sliver of sight we had into the room.

It was Mason.

He was dressed in a suit and tie—his work attire—and he looked official as he moved with determination directly to Adam's desk and began searching through its drawers like he was on a mission. He methodically held up envelopes, ruffled through papers, and then began fiddling with something underneath the desk. I heard rubbing and scraping and then a click. I didn't have a clear view of what opened or what he saw, but he was obviously staring at something.

Once again, the door downstairs opened, and the sound of men's laughter drew closer on the creaky staircase.

Mase quickly shut the drawer and glanced around the room obviously looking for someplace to hide, spotting the door leading to the back stairs. He headed our way, fast. He sprinted across the room on his toes, flung open the door to the back stairs and stood momentarily paralyzed as he found me and Leese scrunched down like two cowering cats on the top step staring back at him with surprise and fear in our eyes. He was only stunned for a second, stepped between us while putting his finger to his lips, and crouched beside me as I pulled the door closed as tightly as I could.

I think we all stopped breathing as the senator and Ad the door swung open the door and strolled into the office talking and laughing.

"Have a seat, son." Ad loosened his tie and dropped into the adjacent chair. The senator was surprisingly handsome, and I could tell immediately he was Mason's father. They had the same penetrating eyes and muscular build, and the same jaw line, but Senator Downes had distinguished salt and pepper hair. I'm not sure what I was expecting, but I think it was someone more along the lines of George Wallace or Howell Heflin—Southern people I'd read about or that I'd seen on the news from days gone by—balding, smoking cigars, and with a deep southern drawl. Obviously, I was out of touch.

Mase and I were scrunched together on the same step with Leese, who was hanging on tightly to the railing, her knuckles visibly whitening. She nudged Mase towards me so she could occupy a bigger portion of the narrow step, but I was already practically in his lap. His shoulder and bicep were supporting us so that we didn't fall backwards. It was stifling in the stairwell with no discernable airflow, and certainly no air conditioning. We all tried to be as still as we could and focus on what was happening just outside our door.

"I'm proud of you, Adam," the senator said, "you've been a true partner in this project, but we need to be very careful. We can't let anything or anyone get in the way of all the sweat that got us where we are. Do you understand what I'm saying?"

He sat back in the chair, removed a pack of cigarettes from inside his suit coat, struck a match and took a long drag. How odd that he was smoking inside; no one smoked inside buildings anymore. No odder, I guess, than me in Mason's lap on a step in a secret staircase.

"I know, sir, and I'm doing everything I can to keep things under control," Ad replied.

"Good. It's almost time to reap what we've sown."

After a bit more small talk, the senator rose from his chair and rested his hand on Adam's shoulder.

"You keep him under control," he demanded, "whatever it takes."

Him?

I wondered why he spoke without an accent. Mason didn't have one either.

"I will, sir," Adam said again.

With that command he left Ad's office, Ad following shortly after.

As soon as we heard them leave, Lisa bounded down the stairs two at a time, through the kitchen to the bathroom that was just off the main foyer, leaving Mase and me alone.

He wasted no time.

"What are you doing here?" he asked, putting his hands on my shoulders, and turning me to face him. His eyes narrowed and his jaw was tense. "You have no idea how dangerous this is." His tone was serious, but I thought he was being overly dramatic. I knew what we were doing was covert, but dangerous?

I ignored the question and responded with my own. "Why? Why is it dangerous? And I could ask you the same thing." I wondered why he was rummaging through Adam's office. "I thought you were out of town."

"I have been. I can't go into everything right now, but you need to listen to me. My father is a dangerous man and Adam is in up to his neck…he stopped mid-sentence as Lisa emerged from the bathroom holding a damp paper towel on her forehead.

"Are you okay?" I asked. She clearly wasn't.

"I'm fine." She patted the paper towel against her red skin. "Look Mase, we're just trying to find some information because I think Adam is keeping something from me. No big deal." It was that plain and simple. At least she made it sound that way.

"And you?" she said. We both looked at him expectantly.

"Business," he said, "now ladies I'm in a hurry, but this conversation is not over. Don't do this again."

With that, he was out the door and gone in less than a minute.

There were no answers for now, and it was understood that we would not discuss this encounter with anyone.

"What do you think Mase is looking for?" I asked, as we erased any evidence of our visit, and began the walk back to my new to me SUV.

She wasted no time to answer. "I don't know, but it's' pretty obvious," she said, "we're on to something."

I couldn't shake the conversation between the senator and Ad, and his instructions to keep "him" under control. I had a terrible feeling in the pit of my stomach.

As we neared my vehicle, it was immediately apparent that my tires were flat. All of them. After closer inspection, we saw that the air stem had been deliberately cut from each tire.

"Who would do this?" I said thinking out loud, not really expecting an answer.

Lisa was quiet as dread and apprehension crept through me.

Chapter 8

Two weeks later I was still waiting for the police report I had reluctantly filed about my slashed tires. Mase flipped when I told him about it a week or so after the fact. He didn't understand my apprehension about involving the police or why I didn't tell him right away. If it wasn't for Lisa's constant harping, I probably would never have reported it or told Mase.

"You don't understand," I said. "Where I grew up everyone handled their own business and involving the police was something no one ever did. Honestly, we never knew what side of the law the police were on."

Even though that explanation was truthful, it was not the entire truth. He and I had not been dating all that long—I didn't want him to think I was the type of person that had tire-slashing drama in my life.

"How were you planning on 'handling' this?" he asked. I could tell he was a little irritated. "And why did you wait until now to tell me?"

It was hard for me to explain because I wasn't used to sharing my feelings or burdening anyone with my problems, and I really didn't want to open the can of worms that was my relationship with my father, or Junior and my "trust" issues, as my therapist called them.

His tone shut me down completely. He sensed this and immediately pulled back.

"Sorry," he said softly, "I am just concerned. I want

you to know you can trust me."

"I'm sorry, too," I offered, "I'm just used to handling things by myself. I'll get better, promise."

He let the discussion end for now. I kissed him on the cheek and headed out the door to the asylum, trying to push the renewed sense of dread created by this conversation to the back of my mind.

****

It was Adam's birthday, and we were supposed to meet him and Lisa later at Flannigans, a favorite sports pub of theirs in Clarksville. Just the name implied I would have fun, and I was excited to get out and have a good time. Well, that, and have a chance to observe Mason and Adam together socially and drinking. Maybe we could get a clue to what was going on with them.

In New York, before we were both married, Leese and I would do our best to end the workday early, have afternoon drinks on her six by eight-foot plant-covered apartment balcony that looked like a jungle, order takeout, and have a Netflix marathon and slumber party. This way we avoided the hotspots and mega bars, also known as tourist magnets. I missed the hurried detachment of living in New York. In retrospect, it was something I loved about city life. You could be surrounded by thousands of people and still have no human contact whatsoever unless you chose it. But it was not this way in Banjoland and it took a bit of getting used to the fact that everyone hugged. Hugging always seemed intimate to me, something saved for those you deem special, but it was different here, and mandatory. There was the frontal for those you knew well, and the side for those you did not. It was part of the culture here and with a little practice I came to embrace it.

On the drive home from work, I had found myself distracted with thoughts about Mase's biceps and how long it had been since I had a been a real relationship. I liked him a lot, and so did Zoey. He was kind and he opened my eyes to a different way of life with a level of sophistication that wasn't uppity, and that made this new world seem okay and fun for me and for Z. He could shoot skeet and kill hogs one day, and put on his suit and tie the next, never changing his personality or attitude.

The best part was his grammar, a huge turn-on for me. And for that I said a quiet thank you to Wes and Olivia Downes. Their money had afforded Mase an excellent private school education, primarily, I would think, to make him a suitable spouse and the appropriate legacy.

"Hey, good looking," said Mase, opening the door to my SUV and reaching for my purse.

Thanks again, Wes and Olivia, for his impeccable manners.

"Hey yourself," I smiled, glad but surprised he was there.

"Thought since the little lady went home with RJ from school, I'd come by a little earlier than we planned," he said.

My heart started beating a little faster, as his afternoon scruff brushed across my face.

Since it was the end of summer, preparations were well underway for hunting season, even though it was still several weeks away. RJ and Ray would be repairing deer stands and grooming food plots, servicing four-wheelers, and making plans. Zoey was in heaven. She loved the outdoors and these activities, and as a pleasant reminder to me and everyone else that she was my child, still applied rule number one and refused to wear camo. She had gone home with him after school to help with these preparations.

Mase opened the door to the house for me and went to the fridge to get us a pre-birthday-party beverage, while I kicked off my shoes and sifted through the mail.

"I missed you today." He popped off the top and poured my lime beer into an icy cold glass and handed it to me.

"Thanks. Funny, I was thinking about you on my way home," I said, and took a sip that tasted better than expected. He sat next to me on the couch and took my feet into his lap, slowly massaging each toe, each arch…

****

Ad and Leese were already at Flannigans when we got there—almost an hour late.

"I texted you," Lisa said, as more of a question than a statement.

"I know," I said, trying to subdue my smile just a tad. "We were occupied."

Lisa rolled her eyes comically as if to say, "it's only sex, it shouldn't have taken that long," but offered a sly grin that said she understood completely.

I was looking forward to an evening of respite, and I could tell right away that I would like this place. It felt normal and reminded me of the abundance of northern Irish pubs in New York City—many of which Leese and I visited during our party days. The lighting was dim, the walls were paneled, and the booths and tables were cozy, leather, and wooden. Irish flags with their, green, white, and orange stripes were randomly dispersed on the walls in between black and white photos and namesakes. The familiar signs for Guinness and Smithwicks hung next to advertisements for Jameson, Tullamore, and Powers whiskey. There was a shield with a family crest on the wall of each booth.

"This place reminds me of . . ."

"McAllisters," Lisa and Ad said in unison before I could get it out.

Mase was rubbing my leg underneath the table when the waitress brought over my pilsner, which I finished in three swallows.

"Let's get this party started," Mase said. "To Adam," he toasted. "Happy birthday, man. And may your son be better looking."

We laughed and held up our glasses. "To Adam."

"Hey, there's Billy Joe and Mark Luke," Ad said, pointing to a group of guys throwing darts. "You in?"

"Let's go," Mase said, and they left us to throw darts with the guys.

"How are you?" I said turning to Leese now that we could speak freely.

"Not as good as you apparently," she said. "You are oozing that new in-love vibe and it's grossing me out a little."

"Don't be jealous." I laughed and took her hand in mine. "You'll always be my first love."

"Yeah, yeah," she said.

The waitress brought another Guinness.

"So listen," she said quietly. "I've been waiting to tell you something," she continued. "I was putting Adam's clothes in the laundry while he was in the shower last night, and when I picked up his shoes to put them away, a phone fell out of one of them and it wasn't his iPhone."

"What do you mean a phone fell out?" I asked.

"Yeah, it was one of those pre-paid phones you get at the Walmart."

This whole thing with Ad was becoming more James Bondish by the day. Having a drop phone was so out of Adam's normal character that I almost couldn't believe it.

"What? No way. You did look through it, right?" I asked, panicking for a moment that her dutiful wife tendency may have overridden her common sense.

"You know I did. I hate that he's hiding things from me, Mel, you know, but he's changed so much since we first got here that I'm not sure who he is anymore."

She nibbled on some homemade chips that our waitress, Stephanie, left with her last beer delivery and continued with a sigh, "They were all from his boss."

"What did they say? What could they be doing that is so double secret they need a phone that can't be traced?"

Not that I was overly surprised, but I think just the confirmation that our suspicions were on target, and something was out of the ordinary with Ad, in fact so out of the ordinary that Mase was stealthily rummaging through his office desk, was disconcerting—I mean a drop phone? I think all along I was hoping that my hunches were wrong or at least misplaced.

"So . . ." The anticipation of what secrets the covert phone held was almost too much for me—in a weird night-before-Christmas kind of way.

"So, I didn't get to read anything because Ad got out of the shower, and I didn't want to get busted and blow any chance we had of finding out whatever we could."

"What did you do with the phone?"

I envisioned her sneakily putting it back in the shoe

exactly the way she found it.

"I put it back in the shoe exactly the way I found it. When Adam got out of the shower and saw that I was picking up his clothes, he made a beeline for the shoes while telling me to take it easy, he would take care of those because, you know, I'm pregnant."

She paused for a moment, then added rhetorically, "Who'd have thought after just a few years of marriage, we would have secrets?"

I never did. In an ineffective attempt to make her feel better I offered a simple, "He loves you."

I sat back in the booth for a minute, gathering my thoughts.

"What about you?" she asked. "Any word from the police?"

"Nothing. Have you said anything to Ad?"

"No."

I thought that was odd—that she didn't share something as significant as this with him—

but I didn't dwell on it because I was preoccupied with Ad's drop phone and what he could be doing that would require one.

Mase waved and gave me the just-a-minute sign with his finger, mouthing "just a minute."

I felt myself smile widely and mouthed back, "No worries."

Stephanie was mingling and feigning pleasantries with the people in the booth next to us—three girls in their late teens or early twenties, dressed in Goth-style clothes and dark make-up—trying to give her their order in what I could only guess was an imitation Irish brogue. Steph faked a smile and worked hard for her tip.

The guys finished their game and returned to the

booth with bragging rights and thirst.

Ad squeezed Leese tightly and kissed her softly on the cheek. "I love you, honey," he whispered before kissing her belly.

As if on cue, Mase kissed me on the cheek and mumbled into my ear, "Many more days like today and you'll never get rid of me."

Ad got Steph's attention while she was navigating the slew of hopefuls playing the game near the bar and signaled her to bring us another round. Poor Leese had to settle for ginger ale.

Within a few minutes, Steph appeared at our table with beers for everyone sans Lisa, and a message for me.

"The guy in the black hoodie at the bar got yours," she said, as she handed me the frosty glass, "and said to tell you that you look as good as you always did."

The dread hit me like a bolt of lightning, and I felt like someone was stepping on my lungs. I scanned the bar immediately. I knew these words and I knew to whom they belonged. The color left Lisa's face. She knew, too.

In the rare honeymoon times when Junior was sweet and charming, usually after a wild romp in the sack, he would talk about us growing old together and that I would look as good as I always did, and he would be distinguished but still hot, and we would laugh like it was a real possibility.

I scrutinized the room. I saw every color scheme and combination, but no black hoodie.

My heart was racing, but I had enough awareness to realize I had to keep it together because there was no way I could explain in a believable way to Mase why I thought my dead husband might be alive. I could hear the conversation now:

"Honey, what's wrong?" Mase would ask.

"Oh, nothing, I just think my dead husband is stalking me," I would explain.

I put that thought out of my mind and excused myself from the table under the guise of using the restroom. Lisa tried to follow, but I didn't wait for her. I felt a little dizzy and the hair surrounding my face was damp with sweat as I weaved in and out of the Friday night crowd, looking for something, anything, that might give me confirmation of what I feared was true. This included a scan of the men's bathroom. Finding nothing but a few strange looks and a crude proposal, I turned to leave and bumped into Mase who had just opened the door.

"Uhm…excuse me?" He looked confused.

"Sorry, wrong door." I offered.

I thought once more about blurting everything to him, but I knew I would likely lose any chance at something solid and long-term with us if I came across as a crazy person, and I wasn't ready to do that yet.

I waited outside for him to finish in the men's room, my eyes inspecting every nook, booth, and shadow, when Steph materialized from the crowd a bit disheveled, and handed her empty tray to another waitress with a few words of instruction.

I practically pounced on her.

"Steph! Steph!" I waved my hand and motioned for her to come over.

She came right over, but politely said, "I'm on a break."

"I don't want to order anything; I just want to ask you about the guy who bought me that drink."

She thought for a moment, "Black hoodie?"

I nodded.

"I can't really tell you much," she said. "I didn't get a good look because, you know, the hoodie. He just left money on the bar after he told me what to say.

"Did I get it wrong?" she asked, "sorry, it's been pretty busy."

"No, I'm pretty sure you got it right. I was just wondering if you saw where he went or if he said anything else, that's all," I replied.

"He was there less than a minute," and then she added, "I don't think you missed anything." She smiled and nodded in Mase's direction. They passed each other as she drifted down the hall, making small talk with the regulars until she left through the back door leading to the alley—I assumed for a cigarette break—and he ambled towards me and pulled me in for a tender kiss. I pulled back before he did.

"I'm not sure what's come over me, but I'm not feeling very well. Would you mind if we just called it a night?"

He stepped back and looked me over, as if he was trying to see if I looked sick.

"Of course. What's wrong? Is there anything I can do to make you feel better?" he said with a wry smile. I knew what he met by "feel better," but I didn't have to answer.

"I'm kidding," he said. "Let me pick up our check and then if we need to stop at a pharmacy or somewhere to get you something, just let me know."

"Thanks, but I just need to get Z and go home," I answered. She had been on my mind consistently as soon as I heard Junior's words and I needed to have her with me, even if I was going crazy.

"Are you sure? Why don't you sleep in and I'll pick her up first thing in the morning," he offered, kindly.

"I appreciate you offering, but I need her with me."

I could tell he wanted to push back on this, but he didn't and while he paid the check, I returned to the booth to get my purse and phone. Ad was focused and texting. Lisa was unusually quiet.

"You okay?" she asked softly as I gathered my stuff.

"No, I'm not. Let's talk tomorrow," I said, confused, and scared and needing to think.

****

It was a quiet ride to Ray and Mary Sue's house. I was consumed by thoughts about Junior and the unfathomable reality that he could be alive. It made no sense, but the words that Steph said, his words, on top of that night at the shotgun wedding when I thought I saw him, were more than coincidences, of that I was certain. I decided to just talk it through with Leese. She and Ad were there that night. They know what happened and that thought calmed me some as I knocked softly on the bolted door.

"What is it, honey? Is something wrong" Mary Sue said when she cracked and peered through the door to inspect her unannounced visitor. She had rollers in her hair underneath a warn hairnet that I could see from the light in the background.

"No," I lied, "It's just that something's come up for us early in the morning and I need to have Zoey with me."

"Well, if you're sure you don't just want to wait until morning. . ."

She gave me a funny look while she unlatched the

door and retrieved my sleeping child from a back bedroom. We transferred possession while Mase waited patiently in the truck.

****

After the longest shower of my life, I dried off, donned my worn t-shirt and a pair of his boxers, and resolved to figure out what the hell was going on. I knew I would have a better perspective once I talked to Ad and Lisa in the morning. I slid into bed, still not used to having anyone there waiting for me.

"So?" he said, lying on his elbow, facing me. "Feeling better?"

"Much," I replied.

"I'm glad," he said, as he pulled me in close, and nuzzled my hair. I liked the feeling of being close to him. It felt safe. I guess that's why I couldn't stop myself.

"Mase, I was kind of freaked out tonight when Steph brough me the beer from the guy in the hoodie."

I need to stop, but I can't.

"How come? I'm sure guys buy you drinks all the time."

"Because those were the exact words that my dead husband used to say to me. And because I thought I saw him that night at the wedding, and because slashing my tires would be exactly something he would do."

I blurted it all out in one run-on sentence hoping if I rushed through it, then it might not sound as crazy as I imagined it would. I held my breath and hoped I didn't just torpedo a relationship that was the first I was hopeful about in a long time.

"I can see why that would freak you out," he replied matter-of-factly, while he rummaged under the covers searching for the tv remote, "but Steph probably misunderstood, and uh, well, he's dead. Was that movie we were watching on Netflix or Hulu?"

He completely dismissed my concern, and I'm not sure if I was glad or annoyed and I wondered what he really thought about my run-on sentence.

"Yeah, of course you're right," I said, and that was that for now.

****

"I get it," Leese responded when I showed up at her house at the crack of dawn. "I've heard him say those exact words to you. Ad says it was just a coincidence, but I can see why it freaked you out."

Ad was at the gym, as he was every morning before the sun came up. Lisa would be there again, soon, too. She said trying to do anything at her stage of pregnancy was miserable.

Lisa sounded so rational. She always sounded so rational. Obviously, I was certainly overreacting.

****

The first time I met Lisa we were beginning middle school. She and her mom had moved to our street the summer just after her parents divorced.

A group of us were jumping rope in the street in front of my house—a daily ritual for the girls in our neighborhood—when Lisa came riding up on her bike. "Let me show you something," she said. Without missing a beat, she jumped into the rhythm of the rope and began a series of jumps and twists that we had never seen before.

We looked on in awe as she recited a new rhyme complete with jump steps we'd never seen before.

"What's your name?" I asked her, as I tried to replicate some of her moves.

71

"Lisa Marie Marcone," she said. "Everyone calls me Lisa. We just moved into the old Harper place."

She was wearing flip flops and I immediately liked her. She was confident, with a friendly vibe and I knew immediately we would be friends.

In the distance I heard the familiar sound of our muffler-less car careening through the neighborhood. The girls scurried around gathering their things and seemingly evaporated in front of us. Lisa didn't move. She didn't know. The ache in my stomach returned, just like every day at this time. I followed suit and grabbed my books and jump rope as my father pulled into our driveway, beer cans spilling onto the concrete, simmering rage beneath his glassy eyes. I left Lisa standing alone in the street as I cowered past my father and into the house. She never mentioned this episode again.

Chapter 9

It was a little past midnight when I crept as quietly as I could across Lisa's front porch. I had kept Zoey close to me since the incident at McAllisters, but she and RJ practically begged, well they did beg, for her to spend the night with a group of kids at Ray and Mary Sue's to celebrate RJ's birthday. I was apprehensive, but as the days had gone by without a further incident and everyone seemed to think these "sightings" were "unrelated coincidences" (Ad's words), I began to wonder if maybe that was true. Mase had gone out of town for a couple of days on business, which I learned was his way of saying he was investigating someone or something and that it involved stakeouts or other private eye-type stuff. I also learned he didn't like the term "private eye."

Now, skulking about in the darkness, I was on edge—like I was about to commit a crime and could be caught at any minute, and wondering if anyone was stalking, I mean staking, me out.

Lisa said she would leave Buddy out back so he wouldn't bark, but I couldn't help feeling like I might get discovered at any minute. I parked down the road a little because, well, that seemed to make sense, and I walked the few hundred yards to their house. I'd given some thought to plausible reasons that I was prowling around Lisa's house near midnight in case I was discovered, but the only remotely credible reason I had come up with was that Lisa needed me and asked me to come over. I hoped I wouldn't have to explain any further because, although I'm pretty quick on my feet, I was at a loss for something to say that made sense. It was a cloudy night, and it was hard for me to see. The crickets were chirping loudly, almost like they were announcing my arrival. I was surprised anyone could sleep.

I did as we planned, sliding across the wooden planks of the porch in my socks, praying to avoid a splinter, toward the corner with the oversized planter where I would wait until Lisa gave me the signal—even though I suddenly realized we didn't discuss what the signal would be. It was very dark with sporadic moonlight sneaking through the passing clouds, but comfortable with a slight breeze. I made a deal with the shadows to keep to themselves and I would not use my emergency flashlight to ward them off and kill them. I slowly eased by the front door, still not fully awake, and accidentally stepped in Buddy's water bowl. I danced around the porch on one foot, trying not to let the other step in what I spilled, keep quiet, and pull off my wet sock, certain I looked like a contorted ballerina.

"What the hell are you doing?" she whispered. "Stop making such a commotion."

It was Lisa, too awake for this time of night, peering around the screen door, fresh with bed head and—so help me—camo boxers and a t-shirt. Even dressed this way she looked beautiful.

"I stepped in Buddy's freakin' water bowl and my sock is soaked," I whispered.

"Okay, grace," she said, mocking my lack of it, "let's get this done before he wakes up and before you wake up Buddy."

"Did you find it?" I asked.

"Oh, yeah. If he is anything, he's predictable. Some things haven't changed."

She produced the drop phone from her other hand.

"We don't have much time. He drank a lot so I don't expect him to wake up, but you never know."

I felt like Indiana Jones must have felt when he was about to obtain the Holy Grail.

We sat next to each other on the steps to the porch, scrunching in close so that we could both see the words on the screen. I swiped across it with my pointer finger, and the spaces for the secret code popped up. Leese took the phone, punched in a combination, and the screen appeared before us.

"Predictable," she muttered.

"Where should we start?" I asked.

"I don't know. Let's just see what the latest text says."

"Okay, here we go."

My heart was racing with anticipation as I expected answers.

I searched for the text message icon and tapped it with my finger.

The most recent text was dated the night of Ad's birthday.

—*Ad: Problem!*—

—*Senator D: Fix it*—

—*Ad: There's been contact*—

—*SD: What?*—

—*Ad: There's been contact*—

—*SD: Goddammit. Meet me first thing in the morning.*—

—*Ad: Yes, sir*—

I exited the text and we sat in silence for a while. In those few exchanges on this balmy summer night in the Panhandle of Florida, we both knew that our lives had changed.

Chapter 10

Lisa came by early the next morning. It was Sunday and Z was sleeping, Mase was still out of town and Ad was at the gym as usual. We had breakfast on my porch, and even though it wasn't as grand a porch as hers, it was cozy and filled with overstuffed furniture that made her look tiny, despite her ever-growing baby bump. It also had a cool porch swing that was my favorite place to think.

"So obviously," she said, devouring a scone and washing it down with orange juice, "because the text came on Ad's birthday at the time we were all together, then the 'contact' must have been with hoodie guy."

"Right," I said, swirling what was left of my coffee and remembering Ad's furious texting when Mase and I were leaving McAllister's, "and his contact was with me. So why would Ad and the senator be texting about someone's contact with me?"

Who was going to say it first?

"He's dead. We were all there and we all saw him. And like I said before, don't you think if Adam knew that somehow, by some act of Satan he was alive, he would have said something? And not only that, why would he be here in Banjoland? And how would he be involved with Senator Downes and Ad? It's not plausible."

It didn't seem like it was when she laid it out like that, so rational. So convincing.

"I know," I said. "I's crazy to even think it, so I was hoping you might have another option that made sense."

Since I left Lisa last night I had tried to come up with an alternative meaning for the texts; but combined with what I saw at the wedding in the trailer/mobile home, and the McAllister's incident, and my slashed tires, I could not come up with anything other than Junior must somehow still be alive. I was hoping Lisa would convince me otherwise.

"I don't…not yet." She took a deep breath and exhaled slowly.

"So why don't we just talk to Ad?"

The air seemed suddenly heavier. I had tried not to let my mind even consider that Junior might be alive, but now I felt like I had no choice. I had so many thoughts racing through my mind it felt like I had competing voices in my head all asking questions at the same time. What if he didn't really die? But we saw him dead. How could he be alive? Why would he be here? Did he follow me? But we saw him dead. How was Ad involved? Senator Downes?

She hesitated for a moment as if she realized the magnitude of what we were discussing and teared up as she said, "no. Because what if we're wrong? What if he's been lying to me?" A single tear streaked down her cheek and fell onto the crumbs strewn across her plate.

What *if* he had been lying to her? What did that mean for me, and especially for Zoey? I vacillated from ignoring the feeling of impending doom that was seeping into my consciousness, to completely dismissing the possibility of this absurd idea.

After a few minutes in deep thought, Lisa wiped her eyes with a crumpled napkin, and threw it onto her plate, resolute.

"You and I are going to continue like we planned," she said firmly. "We'll figure out what is going on, like always. Oh," she added, "and don't mention anything to Mason about this. The least amount of people involved, the better."

Chapter 11

We approached the long cobblestone driveway leading to one of the oldest country clubs in the South driving slowly behind the fashionable cars in front of us. Mase returned from his trip energized and excited about a break he expected in the case he had been working. I was relieved he was back and mulling over how and when to tell him everything, along with Lisa's instructions that we should probably keep what we knew to ourselves. Before I had the chance to come to any conclusions, he shared his own revelation.

"It's no big deal," he explained, "It's been long enough that they've heard about you, so let us just get the formality out of the way. I told them we'd be happy to have dinner with them."

"You want me to meet your parents?"

The thought of meeting someone's parents made me uneasy. I felt like I was on display, which of course, I was, but I decided that I would embrace this brief distraction before Lisa and I took our sleuthing to the next level.

I'd heard stories about the goings on at the "Club" as it was referred to by its members ever since I had moved to Banjoland. There were stories about lavish parties, about secret lovers, and stories about envy. I never would have thought that an outsider like me would be invited to any function at a place like this, but here we were turning into the driveway of the members-only club, made clear by the large "Members Only" sign at the entrance. Mase told me you practically had to be born into membership it was so exclusive. He said the only time he ever went was when he was summoned by his parents.

Mental Note: Discuss with Z the premise of country clubs.

I wondered why we needed to meet Mase's parents here anyway, but he explained that this was their scene. It was where they spent their time, where their friends were, and where their position in society was recognized. I chuckled because he explained it so seriously.

"I'm serious," he said, with a half laugh.

"Got it." I smiled. "I'll behave, promise."

Off to the right of the drive and close to the curb was a smaller sign than the "Members Only" with an arrow guiding deliveries to the back. Each side of the cobblestone drive was lined with lush green, perfectly manicured hedges and magnolia bushes with random blooms of pink and red. The driveway widened as we approached the parking lot. There was a tall, black, steel gate with pointed edges at the top that was attached to a small building, a guard shack I think. It was made of stone; and what looked like leaded glass divided the windows.

We were stopped at the gate since the guard seemed distracted and did not immediately recognize us. He was a smartly dressed, tall black man in a uniform that resembled something a butler would wear, including white gloves. He had a nametag with formal black letters on a gold background that read "Jonah."

Jonah was formal himself as he asked to see

Mason's driver's license and who was sponsoring his visit to the club. Before he could speak, he immediately handed the license back.

"I'm sorry for the delay, Mr. Downes. Please go right through. You know the way."

Mase handed me his license and asked me to put it back into his wallet. It was the only driver's license I'd seen with a good picture on it. There it was again—Mason Westhoven Downes IV – his privilege printed for all to see.

I had prepared to make the best impression that I could, and that included using the last of my Kerastase hair gel for Z and me. The last thing we needed to look like tonight was a piece of broccoli and little orphan Annie. Thanks to the discovery of Tags-On I could have some nice designer clothing at discount prices and unlike Lisa, I was always the bargain shopper despite her criticism that I sometimes dressed like a refugee. My child chose her own clothes adorned with sparkles and bling, as always, and simply asked that I French braid her hair.

Amid Zoey's "oohs and ahs," I took in the entire regal picture. The building was solid stone with iron bars over the windows, similar to the guard shack. It could've easily been situated in a rural countryside in the Old World. What was more interesting to me, aside from how out of place a building like this seemed in this area of the country, was the meticulous detail involved in everything we saw. The grass was perfectly cut in diagonal rows and was a pristine canvas for the golf course in its many shades of green. It was framed by large, healthy oaks. Only the aged cypress trees with their strands of Spanish moss floating lazily and unconfined in the breeze identified the part of the country we were in.

"Take everything that happens tonight with a grain of salt," he said, as he pulled up to the entrance. An older black gentleman opened the door to his truck and helped us out.

And then, there we were, dwarfed by the massive presence before us. We made our way over the cobblestone walkway filled with stones carved with what I realized were founding member's' names. Z and I applied rule number one as we approached the doorman.

"Greetings, Mr. Downes."

"How are you, Simon?"

"Very well, sir. It's good to see you again."

"You, too, man."

"Hi, Mr. Simon," Zoey said, holding out her little hand to shake his, appropriately gloved.

"Hello, little lady," he said, bowing formally.

It couldn't have been more different from New York City if we had been in India.

Mason led us to his family's table. On the way people shouted out to him, and he acknowledged them, but he seemed a little embarrassed by all the attention. Z and I just followed, with him holding each of our hands.

It was easy to pick out which table belonged to his family. There was a lot of activity, people dressed to the nines, stopping by to pay their homage, and to see the prodigal son and his people. It had been a long time since I'd met someone's parents; I felt like I was sixteen.

Mason's mom was just what I thought a typical Southern socialite mother would be like. I guessed she was in her late fifties, but through a good skin care regimen and certainly some injectables, she looked well preserved. She wore a designer cocktail dress, which I recognized as a Mickey Lynn I saw in a *Southern Lifestyle* magazine that Lisa had on her porch. She had a cocktail in one hand and a cigarette in the other. Faux air kisses abounded to those that came by to pay her their dues as she played her obvious role as the dame of the country club society scene.

She had a body that was fit and healthy looking, with light brown hair that she wore swept up with loose ends and a few random curls hanging down upon her shoulders. She had unusual eyes, a purple color, violet, I think—and her face was tan and proportionate. She must've been stunning in her day. But now I could see fine wrinkles I attributed to the smoking, and her skin had kind of a leathery appearance. Maybe it was stress, or tanning, or maybe it was simply the aging process. I had no idea. My mind was filled with all kinds of thoughts as we approached the table. People parted like the Red Sea to let us through. As the commoners divided and his mother came into full view, I could see that she sat in a cushioned chair and was holding her hand out, almost like we were supposed to kiss it. The Godfather had nothing on Mrs. Mason Downes III.

"Hello, Mother," said Mase, taking her hand in his and kissing her on the cheek.

"Hello, son," she said, reciprocating.

They seemed very formal for mother and son. I wondered where their money came from and how she had gained her position at the club. Zoey was oblivious to everything and nothing. She was chatting and socializing with everyone that stopped to chat or gave her an opportunity.

"Mother, this is Lanie," Mase said.

A part of me laughed to myself because I thought with everything I'd seen I should probably curtsey and kiss her ring.

"Olivia Westhoven Downes, of the Atlanta Westhovens," she said, holding out her hand to shake mine.

Olivia Westhoven Downes...of the Atlanta Westhovens?

I was tempted to introduce myself in a similar way, but I didn't think my sarcastic sense of humor would be fully appreciated in this context. Where was Leese when I needed her to enjoy this with me?

Leaning forward, I took her hand in mine. "It's nice to meet you," I said.

I took Zoey by the hand to introduce her. "Mrs. Downes, this is my daughter—"

"My mom and Mase are boyfriend and girlfriend," Zoey said, interrupting.

"So I hear," Olivia said, taking a long drag off her cigarette, followed by a sip from her glass. Her indifference was undisguised.

Mase pulled out our chairs and we sat down in her majesty's circle.

"Mom...Mom!" I felt Zoey tugging on my sleeve and turned away from our less than warm reception.

"What, honey?"

"Can I go over and see that man that's making those balloons?"

I looked over to where she was pointing and saw a clown making balloon animals for what I assumed was a children's birthday party. I was about to tell her no since we didn't know the people for whom he was performing, but Olivia interjected.

"She'll be fine."

She held up her hand and immediately three black men in tuxedos appeared.

"Thomas, take this young lady over to the balloon man, if you would be so kind. Tell Mary Susan it would be a favor to me."

"Yes'm," he said, and took Z by the hand.

She looked at me for my approval and I nodded. Thomas led her over to the balloon man and whispered into Mary Susan's ear. She whispered back, took my daughter's hand, and began introducing her to the children at the party.

I was intrigued by Olivia's command of everyone around her—the staff, other guests, and our table.

Mason excused himself to get our drinks, even though Thomas and his minions were lurking within earshot.

"Tell me about yourself, dear," Olivia said, as required by the guidelines of Southern hospitality.

"Not much to tell," I began. "I'm from New York and moved down South to take a job near my best friend and her husband, who moved here for the same reason."

"Oh yes, the friend…the one that's pregnant."

"Yes."

"Adam's wife," she added, acknowledging the connection.

"Yes," I nodded.

"What about your ex-husband? He didn't mind you taking his daughter this far away from him?"

I thought that was a bit personal, but I answered anyway. Looking straight into her face and taking a sip of my water, I said, "He is dead."

"Oh," she said without a reaction. "Mason didn't

mention that."

I searched through the throngs of people milling about drinking and smoking (still odd to have people smoking inside as it had been outlawed in NY for at least 10 years), wondering why it was taking him so long to return with our drinks until I saw him at the end of the bar talking to his father. They were handsome men, each holding a drink in one hand and a cigar in the other—both at the same angle and leaning just a bit forward as they spoke to each other. Mason was looking intently into the senator's face and the conversation looked serious.

When he glanced momentarily in my direction and our eyes met, I offered a pleading smile and he immediately wrapped up his conversation, dropped his cigar in an ashtray on the bar and beelined towards me.

"So sorry," he said and kissed me softly on the cheek. "I trust you and Mother have broken the ice a bit?"

We both nodded and took a sip of our drinks.

Mason's father joined us after some glad-handing of his own.

"So this is the lovely young lady you've skillfully convinced to be seen in public with you . . ." the senator said, reaching for my hand and lifting it to his soft lips. His cologne was musky and masculine. He was charming and I saw him in an entirely different way than when I was cowering on the staircase.

"Dad, this is Lanie. Sweetie, this is my dad, Wes Downes."

"It's nice to meet you," I said, as he kissed my hand.

"Certainly my pleasure," he said and slowly released his grip. There was something magnetic about his looks, combined with his charm and I realized he was a more distinguished version of Mase. I was engrossed in this moment when Zoey came prancing up to the table with a balloon cat wrapped around her head.

Wes immediately turned his attention to her, scooping her up just like Mason did, and Mase excused himself to go to the restroom.

"Well, young lady, let's see what we have here," he said, taking the cat balloon and placing it on his own head.

Zoey laughed and Wes seemed quite comfortable with her. Olivia, on the other hand, kept smoking and drinking, whispering to her disciples as they came by one by one to check out the commotion.

The sound of my dueling banjos ringtone (when in Rome) caught my attention.

Olivia glanced at me disapprovingly. I scanned the text, thinking it was Leese checking in on how I was surviving my evening, but instead it was from "Anonymous" and it said, "I know where you are."

My chest tightened as I imagined an old horror film where the murderer was calling from inside the house.

"Okay?" Mase whispered in my ear, back from the restroom. He startled me.

I nodded in the affirmative, which was always my go to response.

I had to figure this out and I did think about showing it to Mase right then, but because I already dropped the "I think my dead husband might be alive" bomb on him, I wanted to make sure I laid out my suspicions in a considered, not irrational, way and then I would ask him what he thought. And so I decided to sit on this information until I had a chance to think about it a little bit more, and of course, to chat with Leese.

I finished my drink in one long swallow, and before I had fully set it on the table Thomas swooped in, took it and with a glance in my direction headed to the bar for a refill. I was considerably shaken by this new development, but not enough to let it deter me from finding out what was going on and who was behind these incidents and communications. In fact, it only made me more determined. I would do what I always did and discuss it with Leese. She would know what to do. She always did. And then I would tell Mase.

Our dinner was interrupted by chaos coming from the direction of the club entrance. I glanced up to see several Native Americans dressed in traditional attire scuffling with security and yelling something about Senator Downes and corruption and it "not being over." They were trying to push their way farther into the club but were easily handled by the senator's own personal security team.

"What was that all about?" Mase asked out loud waiting for a response from anyone.

The senator never even acknowledged the disturbance, until the silence begged a response.

"The Indians are just disgruntled over some legislation we got passed," he finally said, unconcerned, chewing on an olive from his drink. "Don't know what's for their own good."

****

I was exhausted by the time we left. So was Z. It takes a lot of energy to monitor every aspect of my behavior, but I didn't think his parents were quite ready for me unplugged. And frankly I was focused on trying to make sense of the entire evening, including the text from Anonymous. Mason tucked Zoey into the back seat, put on her seat belt, and covered her with her Lion King blanket.

We didn't speak until we approached Redneck Central even though I had many questions. He pulled up to the double-wide trailer that was located on the county line that divided the entrance of Banjoland from the City of Clarksville. They sold alcohol, bait, made auto loans, and did tax returns and septic tank installations among other things for the locals. It was called Redneck Central for obvious reasons, and it was where our friends, well most of Banjoland, usually bought their provisions when not shopping at the Walmart.

"I just need to make a quick stop," he said. "Need anything?"

"Alcohol, please."

Zoey was sound asleep in the backseat.

In less than five minutes, he stepped out of the store with someone I immediately recognized. They walked together down the wooden ramp that served as the stairs and stopped for a moment at the bottom. Mase opened three beers with the bottom of his lighter and gave one to Pat, the older Native American from work, took a drink from one himself, and the other I assumed was for me. A few minutes passed. They shook hands and Mase gave Pat a small envelope that he had taken from the inside of his suit jacket.

"Here." He handed me a beer as he slid into his seat.

"What was that about?" I asked, wondering what possible connection Mase and Pat could have, and completely disregarding that Pat was drinking, which I didn't think was allowed given his relationship with the asylum—which I reminded myself I should start referring to by its proper name, the Northwest Florida Human Service Project (NFHSP)—but probably wouldn't.

"Just business," he said.

"Can't you tell me anything at all? All you say is that you are working on something big. I don't need any details; I'm just interested in what you do every day."

"Sorry, hun, no can do," he said, leaning over to give me a soft, lingering, kiss.

"You sound like Michael Corleone in *The Godfather,*" I said half-jokingly and returned his kiss.

"You were fantastic tonight, by the way," he whispered, before pressing his soft lips firmly against mine once more.

Chapter 12

My world was upside down and now included meeting Lisa to secretly peruse Adam's drop phone. I knew this was the key and would eventually give us the information we needed to put all the pieces of this puzzle firmly together.

"I really think I should tell Mase what's going on, Leese."

"Don't you think we should have some facts—something definite—to tell him?

I hadn't told her about the latest text I got at the club, but I was sure when I did she would be completely okay with bringing Mase on-board.

"You show me yours and I'll show you mine," Lisa smiled slyly when we met early the next morning. She vacillated from sadness and worry about what Ad might be doing behind the scenes of their marriage, to invigoration by taking steps to figure it out. I hoped this didn't affect the baby too much.

I shook my head and showed her the text I received from Anonymous.

"When did you get this?" she asked.

"The other night when I was at the Club."

"Okay, this is ominous, and it is escalating. I think you need to show Mase and see what he thinks." She paused. "And whoever this is, knows how to contact you and knows where you are and I don't like it. I think you should tell the police."

Of course, she was right. I would tell Mase as soon as possible.

"Your turn," I said.

We looked at the most recent message she screen shot from Ad's drop phone.

The senator texted, —*Usual delivery tomorrow.*—

"What do you think he delivers?" Leese asked, looking like she was ready to have the baby any day. "And why do you think they text about it on their secret phones?"

"I don't know, but obviously on Mondays Olivia is gone, so probably a good time."

Tomorrow was Monday and it was the regular day Olivia and her cronies spent getting their nails done and massages. I had to be at work, but I knew what Lisa was thinking and I didn't want her to do it alone.

"There's no way you are following him by yourself," I said, expecting her to immediately agree, forgetting for just a minute that was not in her nature.

"Listen," she said, "I'm not an invalid and Adam is my husband. Whatever is going on affects my family, and I'm tired of trying to figure it out this way."

We had been following their texts for days, but they were often covert and difficult to interpret. The most we were able to glean was that Adam delivered something to their house when no one else was home.

In the middle of our conversation about his covert activities, Adam appeared from the back forty acres where he had been playing at plowing. He had bought a 1987 New Holland tractor from the Auction Block, one of his first purchases after they moved here, and sometimes pretended he was a real farmer—a farmer wearing designer shorts, a polo, and a Discount Ammo hat, with no visible dirt anywhere on his body.

"What are you gals chatting about on this gorgeous morning?" he said, stepping onto the porch.

"Girl stuff," we said in unison.

He seemed less stressed lately. Could it be because of the impending birth of his son, or because whatever was going on with the senator had settled down a little?

It was nice to see more of old Ad. They' just finished putting the final touches on AJ's nursery, replete with a moose head the senator had killed on a hunt in Alaska, compliments of the Downes.

"Olivia said not to feel obligated to hang it," Leese told me, "and that a more appropriate gift would follow. Not too long after that, we received this monogrammed silk baby blanket," she said, rubbing its softness against my cheek.

"Banjoland activities this afternoon, ladies," Ad pronounced, pouring a cup of hot coffee into his "Farming is where it all begins" mug. Then he left toward the pole barn mumbling something about okra, with Buddy at his heels. Before Ad was out of sight, Ray appeared from within the usual cloud of dust that engulfed his truck every time I saw him.

"Look, Mom!" Zoey shouted as they bounced into Lisa's driveway, pulled to a stop, and she and RJ climbed out of the back of the truck. Z was spending quite a bit of time with RJ, and she seemed to really enjoy learning the ways of the locals.

I kept Zoey with me most of the time now, but Lisa assured me she would be safe at Ray's too, because "no one messes with Ray," and after a long, detailed explanation of why this was true, I felt she would be safe with him. The only other time she was away from me was when she was at school, and the security presence at the only private school in the area was surprisingly robust. No one could be on campus without an appointment and all the doors and gates were locked. I made a point to meet with the principle and without going into detail, emphasized that no one other than me or Leese was authorized to pick her up.

"What's that on your head?" I asked as Z sauntered towards me like she was a runway model, tossing her head from side to side. Whatever it was, it was furry and it had a tail!

"It's a coon, Mom," she announced proudly, "and I shot it myself. The land provides."

I was speechless. Not in our entire relationship had I ever seen, or even considered, that she would wear a dead animal as an accessory.

"The land what...you what? What?" What kind of supervision was she getting from Ray?

"Grab me a can out of that cooler back there, would ya, girl?" he said to Z.

"Don't get your panties all wadded up, Miss, we was just doing a little shootin' with RJ's .22. She's a good shot, your girl. Should be able to help keep meat on the table, as any woman worth her salt should."

Before I could respond, Zoey bounced over the tailgate, beer in hand, and walked over to Ray, who was leaning against the truck smoking a cigarette.

"Here you go, Mr. Ray."

She wiped the top of the can with the bottom of her shirt, tapped it twice, and pulled open the tab like a pro. I looked directly at her smiling freckled face, wisps of orange clinging to her smudged and sweaty skin from underneath that…raccoon hat.

I reached for my phone so I could add to my video diary of life in Banjoland that I was sure one day would make a good book—and perhaps remind her when she was a teenager that she did in fact where a racoon on her head.

As Ray said his good-byes and I thanked him for dropping her off, he climbed into his truck, hauled out of the driveway leaving a trail of dust lingering behind him and I couldn't help thinking there was more to him than met the eye.

Lisa and I had a few more minutes of conversation so Z could show Ad her kill/hat, and then we made plans to meet later at the hog hunt.

****

"You could've prepared me," I said to Mase, rummaging through my clothes in the biggest closet I'd ever owned.

What does one wear to a hog hunt?

"No worries," he said, "it'll be fun."

Proud of myself for my open-mindedness and "when in Rome" attitude, I ferreted around and found an outdoorsy ensemble with straight leg jeans, boots and a dark green top that tied at the waist. I pulled my hair back with a matching tie, and laughed as I imagined myself wearing it on the cover of *Vogue* as they did their imaginary Banjoland spread. I planned on having "the" conversation with Mase later in the day about the texts. I was apprehensive because I didn't want him to think I was the kind of person who had drama in her life, and at the same time I wanted him to know so he could help, because the person texting me wasn't going away and I was freaking out more than I let on. I'd already told him

I thought my dead husband might be alive and he was still hanging around, in fact, we were getting along really well—I just didn't want to push the envelope.

I asked Mase and Zoey to go on ahead of me to the hunt, racoon hat and all, so I could relax and have a little time to myself. I poured some champagne into my always-chilled flute and took a few deep breaths while I sat on the toilet seat lid waiting for my flatiron to heat up. I missed the City and its familiar detachment. I missed the drone of people and traffic. The food. The life. But something about this place resonated with me. It was different, but something about it was comforting and genuine and for the first time I could see us living our lives here. And now I was going to hunt pigs. I mean hogs, and I was determined to be a good sport.

I stood in front of the bathroom mirror examining my hair and lamenting my need for a trip to a salon when I heard the front door open. We could hear it open anywhere in the house because the original door hinges made a squeaky sound that was unmistakable. Mase kept saying he was going to oil or replace them, but we'd become so used to it that it wasn't a priority anymore.

"Babe, is that you?" I called, setting the brush on the side of the sink and walking toward the bathroom door. "Mase?"

I made my way down the hallway to the living room where I saw that the front door was wide open. There was no way the wind could have done that because there was no wind, and because the door closed so snugly that we had to jerk it hard to open it. No one was around.

The hair on my neck stood up and I stood very still in the strange silence for a moment observing the scene.

I cautiously approached the open door, suddenly

becoming aware of every creak and moan and sound around me. I didn't see anybody. I peered out the front door and stepped onto the porch, hoping to see Mase or Zoey scrambling around with their hands full as the reason for the open door.

Nothing. His truck was gone and so were they.

Thoughts of my slashed tires and the text at the club returned, and I suddenly felt extremely vulnerable. I quickly closed the door, locked it and reached for the loaded pistol Mase kept in the center console of the couch. I remember how absurd I thought this was and how he said that a weapon (not a gun) was useless unless it was loaded. And that every household should have protection. Despite my previous protests and pacifist nature, at that moment I was glad it was there. My heart beat faster as I scoured the house for anything out of the ordinary, pistol held in front of me with both hands, like I'd seen on television.

I vacillated from being scared to feeling like I was in control—I mean I had a gun—and decided in the process that we needed a dog as a first line of defense. I crept down the hallway, entered each room, looking under beds and behind closed doors. Slowly I slinked down the hall toward the bathroom. I felt like I needed to peek behind the shower curtain. As I inched toward it, creepy horror movie music played in my mind until it reached a crescendo as I snatched back the curtain—which revealed a slightly dripping faucet. I was so worked up I almost shot the soap dish.

I set the pistol on the back of the toilet, took a deep breath, finished what was left of the champagne, and resumed my attempts to coif my frizzy do. Without warning there was a tap on the bathroom window. I almost jumped out of my skin. I grabbed the gun off the toilet and spun around to see Ray's face squinting through the frame.

"What the hell are you doing?" I yelled.

"Calm down," he laughed. "Put that gun down and show me where Mason wants the wood left."

I walked to the front door, pissed-off and scared. In my state I could have easily shot him. He wasn't there. I walked to the back door.

"What wood?" I asked as I opened the door to him unloading long pieces of wood and other building material from the back of his truck. I tried to quell my aggravation, now sure it was Ray who had caused the noises I'd heard. I didn't even mention the fact that he was looking in my bathroom window and how that was very creepy.

"For his deer stand. Where should I put it?" He nodded toward a small tin pole barn filled with a couple of tree stands and a four-wheeler. My house was close to Mason's hunting lease, so it didn't surprise me that he would arrange this drop off.

I nodded in the affirmative.

But then I noticed his truck. It was parked behind the house and it was still running.

"How long have you been here?" I asked.

"Just pulled up," he said, and he unloaded a few 2 x 6s, a wooden ladder, and a bucket of nails from the truck bed.

Well, if that was true, he couldn't have been the one that opened my door. He did have a history according to Mase of doing things that were questionable to people he didn't care for, like the times he sneaked into old widow Hanson's house and rearranged her furniture while she slept. Mase said she refused to pay Ray for some work he did to her house because she said he didn't finish it, and he had her thinking she was going crazy. It went on for weeks until Mrs. Hanson's son caught Ray in the act. Suffice it to say that Ray didn't return to Mrs. Hanson's, but he never apologized to her or anyone else for what he had done.

That was an interesting insight into Ray, and I believed he was telling me the truth about when he got to my house. I buried the nagging feeling I had and tried to convince myself I was making a huge deal out of nothing. I took a moment to gather myself, and even though it was still early by someone's standards somewhere, poured another drink.

Mental Note: Get the door fixed and stop looking for things to worry about.

I was startled by the sound of the dueling banjos coming from my phone and when I glanced at the screen and started to panic. It was a text from Anonymous. I held my breath as I slid my finger across the screen to reveal the message: "I can get to you anytime I want. You should lock your doors."

I ran to the back door and flung it open, but Ray was nowhere in sight. That was it. I grabbed my clutch and jumped in my truck. I took off like Dale Jr. speeding away until I felt as if I could breathe again.

I needed to talk to Mase, ASAP. And keep Zoey close.

****

It had been a tiring day at the pigfest, and Zoey fell asleep on the way home. She was sleeping so soundly that she was snoring, and so I took the opportunity to fill in Mase about the texts and my fears about Junior.

He was visibly annoyed that I hadn't shared the Club text as soon as it happened and pulled the truck over to the side of the road in the way that your parents threaten to do on a drive if you don't stop arguing with your siblings and demanded to see my phone. I felt like a disobedient child and handed it over.

He read the text history and sat quietly for a minute.

"This is escalating. First the tires, then the texts. This is serious."

He was certain these things were all connected, and his concern was unnerving and it made me acknowledge my feelings.

"I'm scared," I whispered.

I had not acknowledged that to myself until I said it out loud right then.

"I'm going to dig into this and find out everything I can, Lanie, but you need to trust me. I cannot help you if you don't tell me everything that is going on. Do you understand what I'm saying?"

I nodded. I felt bad for withholding information like this from him, but in my defense, I wanted to avoid the drama in which we were now engulfed.

He took my hand in his and squeezed it gently as he pulled back onto the road.

"And keep Zoey near," he added.

Chapter 13

"Ewe, Mom, gross," said Zoey, dancing into the room still wearing her raccoon fashion accessory, catching me and Mase kissing.

"Not as gross as that thing on your head," I said.

"Mom, I was thinking," she said, "that if we live here for a while, we need to find a good salon somewhere "cause look," she said, showing me her fingernails, and shaking her head.

"These are hideous, and no offense Mom, but nails aren't your strong suit."

Hideous? Strong suit?

"Oh yeah, and Mom, I'd like to have some catfish and cheese grits for supper, please. RJ says that every woman knows how to make those because it's what men like."

Mase chimed in before I could respond. "I'll make you the best fish "n' grits you ever had, little missy, because I think men should cook for their women sometimes, too."

He scooped her up, took the coon hat off her head and put it on his own, and then danced to some country song he was humming that, no surprise, I didn't recognize. When their dance was finished, he set her gently on the floor and gave her some words of wisdom.

"Don't get all your advice on men and women from RJ, sweet girl. He's still got a lot to learn."

"I know," she said. "He's not the boss of me."

She hugged him and danced out of the room humming the same song Mase had been humming. He was so good with her, and it made me love him more. I was glad I told him about the Anonymous texts on the way home from pigfest. Having him in the loop made me feel better...closer to him.

He asked for my phone when we got to the house and made some calls. He said he was using some method the government uses to try and figure out the phone number that correlated with the Anonymous texts.

I felt a little safer.

Our dancing family mood was interrupted by a phone call from Mimi, Lisa's mom. I loved her like she was, well, not my mother, but how I wish my mother had been for us.

"Hi Melanie," she said. She always called me Melanie and her voice made my heart smile.

It wasn't unusual for her to call me. She treated me like she treated Lisa and would call weekly or so to check on me and get the details of my life.

"Sounds like things are going well, honey, but I need to give you some news before I hang up," she said, her tone changing just a bit.

"What, Meems?"

"It's your father," she said.

I didn't respond.

"He died yesterday. He had a massive heart attack."

I didn't know what to say.

"I'm sorry, honey, to have to give you this news. I know you weren't close . . ."

Weren't close? I was disappointed he didn't die when Lisa hit him in the head with the wine bottle that time, or in the car accident, instead of Sissy.

"I mean…I know you two had a difficult relationship. The funeral is tomorrow afternoon, and . . ."

"And what, Meems?" I was certain she was not expecting me to be there.

"I think they're going to bring your mom," she said.

I didn't think you got weekend passes out of Bellevue.

She continued, "And I think you might need to be there, well, because you are the only family that can, you know, make decisions and help her."

"Meems, there's no way I'm going to his funeral. After all the misery he caused our family, I'm glad he's gone."

Those words sounded harsh when I said them out loud, even to me.

"Whatever you think, honey, I know you'll do the right thing. Call me if you need me."

We ended the call and I stared blankly at my phone.

"Lanie, I overheard. I'm sorry. I know you…weren't…um…close…to your dad, but I think you'll be sorry if you don't go."

I let the news sink in for a minute or so before I said anything.

"Listen, Mase, I appreciate what you're trying to do, but I have no intention of going."

"Well, here's what I was thinking," he said. "I don't want to overstep, so please let me know if I do," he continued, ever the gentleman, "but so much that affects you seems connected with your feelings about him. Maybe going to his funeral would give you some closure. Plus…your mom will probably need you."

Closure? Maybe, but I didn't see how. Would seeing him in a casket make him more dead to me than in my mind he already was? And seeing my mom after all this time? No one even told me she was better. I did not want to open all the emotions that would surely come with seeing either of them, dead or alive.

Mase was insistent that this would be good for me.

"Here's what I'm thinking," he explained. "Closure with your dad about everything that happened to you and Sissy. And maybe being able to help your mom might help you come to terms with them and be freeing for you."

Sissy. Sweet, sweet Sissy. She was dead because of him, and I had no forgiveness in my heart. And my mother could have saved us. She could have left him, but she never did. My disgust with her was almost as intense as my hate for him, except on those rare moments when I let myself see her as a victim, too.

"I'll go with you," he continued, "because I know it might be hard."

I'm not sure why this made a difference, because I really didn't want him associated with that part of my life, but the lingering thought that my mother might need me and the crystal-clear memories of her sitting on the living room floor rambling nonsensically and cutting up paper dolls right before she went to Bellevue was the deciding factor.

Everything Banjoland took an immediate backseat to the childhood memories I had tried so hard to assign to a wretched character in a novel rather than acknowledge they were mine. But they we too strong and filled my mind like Niagara Falls pouring into a backyard pool. The senseless unpredictability of my father's moods, the unspoken rules of engagement (acknowledge, ignore, appease, explain) and you had better choose correctly. The rage, the tears the terror. Sissy clinging to me as we hid in my bedroom closet, whispering words of comfort, hoping to avoid the worst. Sometimes, on a day our grandma was watching from heaven, it worked.

"Lanie, honey. . ."

I felt his hand on mine and in an instant I was returned to the moment.

"Yes, I should go. Of course."

"If you would like, I can arrange for Zoey—"

"She's coming with us.´ I cut him off, sharper than I intended. "Sorry. I didn't mean to sound so snippy."

"You got it," he said without argument.

****

Ah, the City. I was home. Even the air smelled different in SoHo. People everywhere, moving at breakneck speed to get wherever they were going, cabs weaving in and out of traffic. The early autumn colors dotted the city canvas. How I missed it.

"Mase, I know you've been to New York a few times, but never with a born and bred home girl. I wish I had time to show you all the cool places—the places that only locals know."

"Next time."

"There she is! Meems!" Zoey yelled, and broke free from my hand, weaving in and out of the river of people approaching until she jumped into her arms.

We arranged to meet at a café a few blocks from St. Mary's because there was no way I was making a trip to the City without seeing her in person. I hugged her tight and for a long time. She looked and sounded so much like Lisa.

"My sweet Melanie. I've missed you, dear. And Zoey, why you're practically a teenager."

I missed her so much. Without her and Leese I never would have survived my life. I introduced her to Mase and we had a leisurely lunch spent catching up until it was time for good-bye and for us to make our way to the main event. She graciously offered to take Zoey to a local salon for the full treatment, as she called it, because she said funerals were no place for children. With Zoey promising to be on her best behavior and my shoulders 50 pounds lighter for not having to guide her through whatever might happen, we paid our bill and I began to mentally prepare.

Our cab pulled up to St. Mary's and dropped us off next to the old blue and white bus that used to take us on field trips when I was a kid. Everything was so familiar, but I was detached and numb, my tried-and-true survival skills.

"I don't want to stay for the service. I don't want to hear someone who didn't know him sing his praises and talk about what a wonderful man he was."

"I understand. Why don't you just go in and pay him a visit alone and then we'll go?"

I was sure Maryann would be here. She was the only friend I think my mother ever had. I just didn't think I could bear seeing my mother as what she had become—listless, fragile, hollow.

We walked up the steps to the church holding hands. As we entered the large wooden doors as I had so many times before, I was overwhelmed once again by the smell of flowers. It reminded me of Sissy's funeral. The memories of her little casket covered in lilies brought tears for her that I didn't want anyone to confuse as tears for him. I composed myself as we entered. The church was empty except for the casket in front of the pulpit flanked by large floral arrangements on both sides. I was surprised at the number because I didn't recall him having many friends. Relatives probably sent them. Mase offered to accompany me to the front of the church, but I felt like if I was going to do this at all, I needed to take these steps alone.

I dipped my hand into the holy water perched as usual in a glistening gold bowl right inside the door to the sanctuary and made the sign of the cross as I had been trained to do so many years ago. I slowly made my way down the center aisle until I was standing over the person who had affected me so deeply. His wide sideburns and the crescent shaped scar on his chin from the accident with Sissy still hadn't changed. He looked older and grayer, but essentially the same.

I felt nothing as I stared at his lifeless body. I had waited such a long time for this day, the day we…I… would be finally free of him for good. But I had become so practiced at acting like I had no emotions when it came to him that I had none for this monumental moment.

So, I sat down on the front pew and wondered what my life would have been like if I'd had normal parents. I stared at his body resting on the red silk lining of the casket. He was wearing the suit I had only seen once before, at Sissy's funeral. This remnant of a life showed no trace of the mean, perverse man I had known. It didn't matter because I knew who he was and the number of flower arrangements or a lovely eulogy wouldn't change that. Our lives should have been different. Sissy died because of him, and I had been an emotional train wreck that married a younger, handsomer version.

Had he ever thought about what he was doing and the way he treated us? I never could make sense of it.

If Mase thought I'd have some type of catharsis, it just didn't happen. I didn't forgive my father. I didn't cry. I didn't beg and plead for acceptance and love. I felt nothing. I got up from the pew, glanced one last time at the man who had been our alpha and our omega, and realized that I had a new beginning waiting for me just down the aisle.

As I turned to leave this anti-climax, I noticed Father O chatting with Mase in the vestibule. My mother was with them…deep breath…one last hurdle before the finish line.

"Father," I said, giving him a huge hug, genuinely happy to see him. I was always happy to see him.

"Ahhh, Patty," he replied. "You haven't changed one bit."

He had called me Patty since the first time we met. Said I needed a nice Irish name to go with my freckles (had them when I was a kid) and sunny personality.

"Hi, Mom," I said, trying to disguise my shock at seeing her.

"Jesus, Melanie, you could at least give me a hug."

We never hugged, not one time in my life that I can remember.

I gave her the awkward side hug, the kind you give someone that you don't know very well, but you know well enough that some kind of contact is expected, thankful that I had learned this option in Banjoland.

"Where's Maryann?" I asked, feeling pressured to make conversation and still stunned to see her.

"Parking the car," she said flatly.

She looked better than she looked before Bellevue. She was alert and didn't have that fragile, anemic look I'd become used to. Her dishwater blond hair was neatly smoothed into a ponytail, and she was wearing a black pantsuit that flattered her trim figure. She didn't need help walking or standing, and she was coherent. She looked almost normal.

"I take it you two have met?" I said, squeezing Mase's hand and nodding toward my mom.

"Yep," Mase answered, squeezing my hand in return. "I was just telling your mom about Zoey's latest kill."

"You must be proud," she said sarcastically.

"So, Mom," I said, ignoring her comment and changing the subject, "you look really good. How are you?"

"I live in a mental hospital. How the hell do you think I am?" she answered.

I was taken aback for a minute. I never remembered her speaking this sharply.

"They say I have some anger issues. Imagine that," she said.

I was embarrassed by her and I didn't understand why. She was my mother in whatever capacity she had been capable of being a mother. It was during long needed therapy I began after Junior died when I first realized that she suffered just as much if not more than Sissy and I did at the hands of my father. I used to think she was complicit and weak. Sometimes I still did. My opinion had softened over the years about almost everything in life, except where my father was concerned. I was as furious with him dead as I was when he was alive, despite my efforts at ambivalence. I thought about my family and Mase's family and chuckled to myself as I thought about introducing my mother to the Downes at some family event. "Olivia of the Atlanta Westhovens, meet my mother, Joan of Bellevue."

"I have to say I'm surprised you're here," Joan said, interrupting my thoughts. (I always referred to her as Joan rather than Mom.) No one hated that bastard more than you did."

"I thought you might need me," I said, immediately feeling small and realizing how ridiculous that must have sounded to her.

"Sure," she laughed, "I might need you."

After a few more minutes of small talk, we left as the church started filling with people.

Mase flagged a cab while I tried to figure out if that woman I was talking to was a glimpse of my future.

"I'm proud of you," Mase said as the cab whisked us away.

I smiled but didn't speak.

I turned on my cell and it dinged as I took it out of silent mode. There were a few texts from work and one from Leese. I was relieved that none were from Meems, which meant that all was good with Zoey. Lisa's text said that she had some info and I needed to come over straight from the airport.

Chapter 14

We landed on time, and as planned, headed straight for Lisa's house. Z chattered on about food plots, tree stands and something about using odor-free Tide to remove the human scent from our clothes—things she had read in a magazine we picked up in the airport called *Sportsman's Guide*. Mase had driven to the airport separately because he was working on a blockbuster case that he thought would be coming to trial soon, so he went straight to work. He also said he might have a lead on Anonymous.

Lisa was on the porch waiting for us. "Hey, girls," she said and bent over as far as she could to hug Zoey.

"Hey Aunt Leese," Z said, hugging her round belly. "Meems says hello." She then bounced into the house, grabbed the TV remote from its familiar perch on the end table, and turned-on Nickelodeon. Buddy made room for her on the overstuffed living room chair.

"Okay," I said, taking a long drink—I finished half of it right away— of the cold limey beer she set before me, "give me the scoop."

"First," Leese said, "how did it go?"

"Your mom was great as usual," I answered, producing the cannoli she demanded I bring back with me.

She nodded, opened the wax paper delight, and waited for me to answer her question.

"It was fine," I said. "He's finally dead. But interestingly, Joan was there."

Her eyes widened.

"Your mom was there?"

"Yeah. She looked surprisingly good. I spent about five minutes with her at the church and then we left for the airport."

"Good for you," she said, sucking out the cheese filling of her pastry.

"Okay, now tell me what's going on," I said, ready to change the topic of conversation.

"Well, we both knew I would follow him, didn't we?" she said, as more of a statement than a question.

"Of course," I said, taking another drink.

"Adam left around his regular time, so I figured I'd drive over to the senator's house and get into position."

"Get into position?"

She continued, "They're doing construction in that neighborhood. Building a house across the street and about half a block down in that empty lot," she said, "so I just parked my truck next to all of the other trucks working on the site."

"And no one noticed the pregnant lady?" I asked, quickly finishing the last of my beer.

"Not surprisingly, no, because they were all in the house working, no one paid any attention to me on the sidewalk. I knew there was a gate on the fence that ran along the side of the house, between those two huge azalea bushes leading onto the deck. Adam and I had used the same gate to sneak out of the senator's re-election party without being noticed. From there someone can see directly into the senator's office, if his blinds are up, and I figured for sure that's where Ad would be. What I saw is burned into my brain."

"And?"

Lisa let my anticipation build before she let her bomb drop.

"It was Olivia," she said.

"Olivia?"

"Yes. She was not at the club as we expected. She was in the pool."

She held up her phone to show me a pic she had taken.

"Oh my…who is that with her?"

"It's the guy that works for Senator Downes that wears the dark sunglasses."

"I can't believe it. She was naked in the pool with Sunglasses?"

"What did you do?" I asked, visualizing this scene in too much detail.

"Well," she said, "I tried to look away, but it was like a car wreck, you know? You don't really want to see the gory details, but you just can't turn away. I knew you wouldn't believe it, so I took a picture just for you with my phone."

"Damn."

"I know." she said and looked at the image again. "She looks fantastic."

She did.

"Send this to me."

I wasn't sure why I wanted it, but I did.

"Okay," she said, and forwarded the compromising picture to me. She continued, "I felt weird watching them, and I thought when Adam showed up Sunglasses might make a quick exit out through the gate and I would get busted."

"Good thinking."

"So I figured I'd leave. At least we know the schedule."

"Yeah, that was probably the best idea." I couldn't imagine how she would have explained herself if she'd gotten caught anyway.

I hadn't told Mase about Leese and me conducting our own investigation into Ad's activities. I justified that by reminding myself that he had his own big case happening and he was helping with Anonymous—I mean, he had a lead! No need to distract him until if/when we found out anything of value.

****

Despite everything that was happening, Mase encouraged me to try and keep our lives as normal as possible.

"How do we live 'normally' with everything going on?" I wondered out loud.

"When was the last time you went shopping, you know— what did you call it? Oh yeah, have a 'girl's' day?

He thought that would be an excellent distraction, as did I when I realized I hadn't had a proper shopping experience in what seemed like an extraordinary amount of time.

"Yes!" I exclaimed, with unanticipated excitement. "Excellent idea, Mase."

I gave him a quick kiss on the cheek and texted Leese to get ready. I chose Tallahassee as our destination because it was the closest, largest city, so we could have an enriched shopping experience. Shopping in Banjoland consisted of visiting the Walmart, Redneck Central, and a few Dollar General stores. There was new excitement in town because there'd been talk about a Target opening up next year. And while that was fine for daily needs, a true shopping day needed to afford us with options.

"Mom! Mom! Let's go to a real salon and get a mani-pedi," Zoey chirped and climbed, along with her Hello Kitty purse and matching pink flats, into the back seat of my SUV. "I need a fill-in."

Lisa, in an unusually upbeat mood, considering how large and spongy she had become, added, "Yes, I need someone to rub my feet and do my nails."

"Yep. No offense, Aunt Leese, but your nails need work."

"I know, girlfriend, I know."

I blasted the air conditioning, we applied rule number one, and off we went on our adventure to the city. It was just like old times, except everything was different.

After making four stops on the way for Lisa to pee, we finally entered the Tallahassee city limits. First item on the agenda was to eat. Lisa and Zoey were both likely to get cranky when hungry, so we were going to head that off first thing. We found a trendy pub in the downtown area near Capital Circle that had tables outside on a patio next to the sidewalk. It was a perfect place for us to people watch and eat.

Zoey hit me up for some pennies to throw into the fountain adjacent to the pub, and that left me and Leese alone to talk.

"How are you?" I asked her. I was so glad to have her in my life on a daily basis again despite all of the chaos.

"You know, I'm okay, Mel," she said thoughtfully. "I really am."

I believed her. She was a tough cookie.

"I'm looking forward to AJ getting here, and as for Adam, whatever is going on, I'm sure he'll do the right thing."

She seemed confident, even peaceful about it.

We had our nails done—mine in French tips, Z and Leese got some trendy green pea color— shopped at baby boutiques for AJ and bought Zoey a lip gloss ten-pack. It was restful and fun and good for us.

"I'm glad you're here," Leese said on the drive home and took my free hand into hers.

"I know it takes getting used to, but it can be a pleasant way of living, in Banjoland," she added.

Lisa and Zoey both fell asleep on the ride home, leaving me alone with my thoughts. Lately it seemed whenever I got a quiet moment they inevitably drifted back to Junior or my mother. *Could he really be alive? I shot him. Joan is crazy. What if I end up in a mental institution just like her?* Despite the excitement of being in love, taking care of Z, working and everything else, these competing narratives were continuously running in the background of my mind, like an old warn out recording waiting for a moment of silence to be heard.

****

When I pulled into Lisa's driveway it was obvious something was wrong. Her front door was slowly swinging back and forth on one hinge, squeaking in the slight breeze.

I got out slowly, eased my door shut but didn't fully close it so I wouldn't wake up my sleeping passengers, and took a few steps toward the porch.

I crossed the wooden planks until I stood in front of the open doorway and saw what I can only describe as what I think it looks like after a tornado hits a house. It was completely trashed; I was freaked out.

I fumbled with my phone trying to dial Mase as quickly as I could. I wanted him to be here when the police showed up.

"Get back in the car right now," he said. "I mean it, now. Lock the doors and wait for me. I'll call the police."

I complied while I nervously looked around for something or someone unfamiliar or sinister. The sound of the old rusty windmill slowly churning in the breeze against the backdrop of the sun fading into dusk seemed eerily out of a horror movie.

In what I was sure was record time, Mase pulled up followed by some unmarked cars, with Ad skidding in behind them. The chaos woke Lisa and despite my efforts to keep her situated, she opened the door and headed out. Mase motioned for us to stay put and entered the house with his colleagues and Adam. I kept the motor running to keep the air conditioning on while we sat in my truck and waited, and while Zoey slept.

Eventually they came out, single file, a couple of them removing thin rubber gloves from their hands. Ad was pacing back and forth across the porch while puffing on a cigarette. The tallest of them was brushing dirt off his creased pants and another was on his phone. Mase signaled Ad to follow him as he came over to us and we got out of my truck to talk to him.

"I think it's a good idea for you two to stay with Lanie tonight," he said to Leese and Ad. "Your place is trashed, but it doesn't look like anything was taken, although you'll have to confirm that. We can fix the door so that it shuts, and we can come back tomorrow and clean up."

He didn't leave room for discussion.

Lisa nodded. I thought she was doing a good job of holding it together. Ad didn't say much; he was intently listening to Mase and the other men, absorbing everything.

"I just need to get a few things, and Buddy," she added and pushed past Adam toward the door.

He stepped in front of her. "Let Lanie do that for you. I don't want the mess in there to upset you more than you already are. I know it's been a long day."

She looked at him for a minute, as if weighing her options, then resigned that she really had no choice, walked back to the SUV, and leaned against the door.

"Fine," she said.

Mase turned to me and then Ad. "Come with me inside for a minute and I'll help you." He took me by the hand and nodded Ad toward the door.

As soon as we got inside the ransacked house, he said, "The people who did this are dangerous, and were obviously looking for something. Do you have any idea what it might be? Lanie? Adam?"

I had no idea and said so.

Ad was also silent.

"I'm serious. Think hard. These people aren't playing around. Lanie, have you received any other texts or anything out of the ordinary or unusual?"

"Nothing at all," I replied.

"No, man," Ad said as well, "I can't think of anything."

Mase shot him a glance like he knew he was holding out, but he didn't directly confront him. Ad glanced at the floor without saying a word.

"Okay, Lanie," he said, more softly now, turning his

attention to me, taking both my hands into his, and looking straight into my eyes. "Go get Lisa some clothes." He looked over at Adam, who still seemed a bit shell shocked by the disaster scene in front of him, and said, "I'm sorry, Adam, about all this. Lanie…Buddy is dead. He was hanging from the oak tree in the backyard. We buried him so no one would have to see him like that."

"What?" I immediately turned to face the back of the house and the oak tree.

Ad's eyes watered.

"What?" I said again, shaking my head in disbelief. I pictured Buddy's stiff black Labrador body hanging by a rope around his neck swinging back and forth in the breeze.

I started to cry. Sweet Buddy. Why would anyone do this?

"This is how we know they are serious," Mase said to me. "They did all this to send a message."

Ad wandered through the open door towards the oak and fell onto his knees over the mound of fresh dirt, running some of it through his fingers as if he was verifying Mase's story. His head collapsed into his hands.

This was bad.

We let Lisa think Buddy ran off but I'm not sure she believed us. He just never did that, and Ad was barely composed, making some excuse about his allergies acting up.

Whoever did this was obviously looking for something, and it was also clear, at least to me, that Ad seemed to know more than he was telling.

The next morning was Sunday, so I dropped Zoey

off at Sunday school and headed over to Lisa's to help with the cleanup.

Nothing had changed since the night before. Everything was in disarray: broken picture frames, dishes in pieces, clothes scattered everywhere. I guess I was hoping that maybe it wasn't as bad as I initially thought. It looked like whoever did this did their best to make the biggest mess possible. Lisa gasped when she stepped through the broken door into her living room for the first time and stood motionless as she surveyed the damage.

"Who would do this?" she asked to no one, slowly looking over her broken and damaged possessions.

"Well, to figure that out, first we need to know if anything is missing," Mase said.

"I had Adam's mother's engagement ring and a pair of diamond earrings and a diamond necklace in my jewelry box, plus a few other valuable stones," she said. "I guess I should see if they're still here."

I held her arm to help her balance as she stepped over a couch cushion and around a busted lamp and strewn newspapers and magazines into her bedroom. All the drawers of each dresser were pulled out and scattered over the floor, contents spilled out, except for two on the bed. Lisa went straight to the jewelry box, which still contained all her valuables.

She exhaled and tried to hold back tears that were developing in the corners of her eyes.

I held her closely as she stopped fighting them.

"It's okay," I whispered, stroking her hair and thinking about what to do next.

Just then I felt a slight poke in my stomach. I stepped back from Lisa as she took my hand and put it gently on her belly. After a few seconds I felt it again. AJ was kicking. We sat on the bed, and she lifted her oversized top so I could see the outline of his tiny foot pressing against her tight skin. She rested my hand on the same spot, with hers on top of mine, and he began to roll and turn and push. I was amazed at this life inside of her. I felt him. I felt his life.

"Does it hurt when he does that?" I asked her.

"No," she said. "It feels like bubbles, kind of, and well, like someone pushing on you from the inside out." She laughed and wiped her tears.

Mase appeared in the doorway to check on our progress.

"It's awfully quiet in here," he said. "What did we find?"

"They didn't take anything of value," she said, pointing to the jewelry still in its place in the box.

"I thought that would be the case," he said, as he sat next to us on the bed.

"Lisa," he said in the same direct way he asked me, "do you know what they could've been looking for?"

"I have no idea," she said.

"Are you sure? Think," he said.

I got up and walked over to the window. Ad was pacing in the driveway, cigarette in one hand, cell in the other. He was gesturing with the cigarette, emphasizing whatever he was saying, like the person on the other end could see him.

I turned from the window and let the curtains reconnect.

"Let's get this mess cleaned up," I said, and we began returning the dresser drawers to their appropriate place.

It took several hours to get things back to as normal as we could.

I took the last bag of trash out the back door and to the can. My heart sank when I saw Buddy's water bowl and I couldn't stop spontaneous tears from running down my face.

I spent a few moments outside so Lisa wouldn't see me lose it. My heart ached as I continued to picture Buddy hanging from the tree. I tried to counter those thoughts with others about AJ and my experience touching him. I was starting to get a migraine.

Mase opened the back door after me and struggled not to drop the ripped cushions and lampshade he was carrying to the can. He lost his balance, tripped down the few wooden porch steps and fell face first into the cushions. I busted out laughing, and when I leaned over to help him up, he pulled me onto the cushions with him. He hugged me in a way that made me feel safe and I relaxed just a little. He kissed me deeply and with such passion that I was unexpectedly aroused. He leaned up and brushed the hair from my eyes.

"I love you, you know," he said softly.

"I love you, too." I did. I genuinely loved him.

He kissed my neck and we both lay there for a few moments enjoying the distraction when we heard muffled arguing coming from somewhere in the front of the house.

We leapt to our feet, adjusted our clothes, and silently crept along the bushes in the stealthiest manner we could, until we were almost to the front yard. Lisa and Adam were arguing, albeit in a loud whispered tone, but it looked intense. Her face was red and she was demanding answers.

"I need you to tell me once and for all what is going on," she said, "I can't live with the secrets and veiled comments anymore. If you don't trust me enough to clue me in, then I'll make a different plan for me and the baby."

I never heard her speak to him like this. Even their most heated exchanges were respectful and non-threatening.

Ad looked panicked. Before he could reply, Mase howled and flung his hand back and forth until the winged creature that had latched onto it was on the ground and stomped to death with enough force to kill a small animal. He looked like he was doing an Irish jig. I dodged his flailing arms and his death stomp, but the ruckus immediately gave away our covertness. We scrambled together into the yard, swatting real and imaginary wasps, and their conversation disintegrated immediately.

Chapter 15

I dropped Z off at school and proceeded to work as usual the next day despite everything that happened over the weekend; I was relieved to get back into my routine. Pat was mopping the hallway.

"Morning, Pat."

"Ma'am." He ran the mop along the baseboard. "How are *you*?" emphasizing you, like he knew something.

He stopped mopping to make eye contact.

"I'm okay, why?" I asked.

"No reason," he said, and returned to his task.

That was odd. I fumbled with my keys and entered my office.

A pile of mail was stacked neatly on the corner of my desk, thanks to Mark Luke. He had the organizational skills of royal staff. He said I could thank his father the Baptist minister.

"Chaos is sinful," he'd say, "of the devil."

I laughed about how he said that, but I appreciated how much it benefitted me, nonetheless.

I started to peruse the stack when I noticed a small envelope about halfway through the pile that resembled an invitation or thank-you card.

The handwriting was like you would expect from an older person, squiggly lines and uneven characters, and oddly, it didn't have a stamp on it. It was addressed to me and I took the NY Yankees letter opener that I use to create conversation and sliced open the sealed flap.

The envelope contained two pictures. One was of Z in her bathing suit in water up to her neck wearing her coon hat. She was in Ray's pool. The picture was a close-up, so close you could see the freckles on her pink face. All you could see was her and water, nothing else. My stomach tightened.

The other one was a picture of Buddy hanging from the big oak tree in Lisa's back yard. I gasped and threw the pictures on my desk. My brain was schizophrenically flashing scenes of my life across my mind: Z, Buddy, Junior, my parents…Things were escalating and I was thinking that maybe we should return to SoHo. I called the police, and they said they would investigate but I couldn't shed the anxiety and darkness that I felt envelope my soul.

****

Zoey was chatting in the tub about how Banjoland needed a spa.

"Maybe Mr. Ray can build one, ya know, like their pool," she chattered.

Every time I heard her talk like this, of spas and nails and clothes, she reminded me of myself, and I loved it. Since she didn't look anything like me, whenever she spoke or acted like this, I took a moment to savor it.

It was also offering a periodic distraction from the most recent discussion I'd had with Mase about the pictures, and about everything, all of it, and the genuine look of concern on his face because things seemed to be headed for a climax. He hadn't been able to find out anything about the texts, like he thought he would, other than they appeared to come from a pre-paid drop phone.

He didn't like how persistent this person was or how close we now knew he had been to Zoey. He was going to do a full-blown investigation, call in "the best to find out what was going on," but in the meantime, he said I should keep Zoey with me, avoid being alone and even though I wasn't used to it, to keep him informed of where I was all the time.

"I can't protect you if you're back in SoHo," he added after I mentioned that option. "And as soon as I can I'm going to put a guy on you, you know, to look out for you. Should take a day or two," he'd said and left to take care of some business, saying he would be back shortly.

"And you know what else, mom?" Z continued, washing her hair into a soapy spike on top of her head and bringing me back to the present.

"What, babe?"

"RJ says that girls should get married, have babies, and cook for their men."

"That's interesting," I said, picturing these exact words coming out of Ray's mouth.

"And you know what I said, Mom?"

She didn't let me answer.

"I told him he better wise up ''cause girls can do anything they want to do and maybe my husband will cook for me!"

Being in her presence made me happy.

I dried her off, helped her get her jammies on, and slathered on her "beauty cream" (moisturizer from the Walmart). Lisa had convinced her since she was old enough to comprehend it that you have to protect against wrinkles from the day you are born.

The last part of our ritual was her bedtime story

about the creatures of the forest. It was a story that I made up and added to every night. The characters were children on a never-ending adventure in a forest.

"Mom, it's not plausible that children can live in the forest alone."

This kid.

"It is plausible if the forest is magic."

Once I had her tucked in, I took my usual place on the couch, relieved and confident that Mase would protect us and get to the bottom of everything. I flipped through the TV channels looking for some good background noise while I began my latest novel and waited for Mase to finish working and pick up some take-out. Before I could get completely comfortable and open the book, someone knocked at the back door. My cell rang at the same time.

That's odd. Hardly anyone uses the back door.

I ignored the phone and opened the door.

Before it was completely open, Junior bolted through, grabbed me by the neck, and slammed me into the kitchen wall.

"Thought you could just blow me off, did you, bitch?"

I was confused and shocked, but not as shocked as I should have been because somewhere not so deep down, I knew it was him at McAllisters, and then I knew it was him behind the texts, and I was just hoping Mase might prove me wrong.

"Junior...I thought...I thought . . ."

"You didn't think I was going to let someone else have you and my baby, did you?" He squeezed my throat tighter. I almost couldn't breathe.

"You think you can shoot me and leave me for

dead?"

His eyes were glassy and he stank of alcohol.

"Junior, I . . ."

"Shut up," he growled and slapped me hard across the face.

I didn't make a sound even though it stung badly. I didn't dare wake up Zoey.

My cell phone rang again.

"Junior," I said, trying to remain calm despite my panic, and calm him, "I'm really sorry about everything."

"I told you when you pointed that gun at me that I should kick your ass," he said. "Imagine what I'm going to do to you now because you shot me." He slapped my face again, this time so hard my nose started bleeding.

My cell rang again.

"And that dumbass Adam. I never liked that bastard anyway," he spewed. "Thinks he's some bigshot working for a senator. Pieces of shit, both of them."

I caught that piece of information and filed it for later, but Junior was angry and volatile, and I was focused on protecting myself and Zoey.

"I want to see her," he ordered. "I want to see my girl."

Hearing him call her his girl made me sick to my stomach. I didn't think he'd hurt her, but he was drunk and irrational, and I was vulnerable and scared.

My cell rang again. This time I made a move to answer it.

"Don't touch it or I'll blow your head off."

I turned to see him pointing a pistol at me.

"Junior, please," I said, as the phone became silent. "She's asleep. Why don't you come back tomorrow when she's awake?" I offered, not meaning it of course, but trying to buy some time.

He took a step towards the hallway and I tried to block him, but he pushed me aside and continued towards her bedroom door. I jumped on his back. He stumbled forward, dropped the pistol, and we both fell onto the floor.

He laughed.

"You think you can stop me? I'm gonna see my baby and then you're gonna pay for shooting me," he growled, the alcohol stench from his breath permeating the room. He wrestled me off of him and went to pick up the pistol that had slid toward the recliner.

That was it for me. "No, Junior, no you're not." I was quiet and determined.

"I don't know who you think you're talkin' to," he snarled. He forgot about the pistol for a minute and grabbed me in a bear hug from behind so I couldn't move my arms. He dragged me across the floor and threw me onto the couch.

"I'm the boss, got it? One day you'll learn to keep that big mouth shut."

"Junior, please . . ." I begged.

"Please?" he mocked. "Oh, you want me, don't you? Say it! Say you want me!"

He pinned my hands over my head with his knee on my pelvis.

"You do look as good as you always did," he added, eyeing me up and down. He kissed me on the mouth and I turned away.

"Junior, stop, please," I said softly, still aware of Zoey in the house.

"I like it when you beg," he said.

I knew what was coming next, so I did the only thing I could and threw all my weight at him until I was no longer on my back. He wrestled with me to try and get back on top, but we rolled onto the floor. He put his knees on my arms while he unzipped his pants.

"I told you before that you would always belong to me, and I'm gonna take what's mine."

I couldn't move my arms because his knees were cutting off my circulation, so I tried to use my knees to kick him in the back.

He tore my camisole, exposing my breasts, and then he reached for my pajama bottoms.

"John Robert! No!" I thought using his formal name might get his attention, but it didn't.

I was as forceful as I could be, but he was so much stronger, even drunk, that there was little I could do to stop him.

"Please. Please don't do this. If you ever loved me, I'm begging you please don't do this."

He stopped for a minute with a quizzical look on his face, like how could I doubt he ever loved me?

The break only lasted for a few seconds though, and he snapped back to what he was doing and pulled my pajama bottoms off.

I braced myself for what I knew was coming, but when he let go of one of my arms to take his underwear off, I punched him in the crotch. He fell backwards and I managed to sprint to the front door. I opened it quickly, but he grabbed me by the hair and pulled me back into the house. He punched me in the stomach and when I bent over forward, he rammed his knee into my nose. Blood was dripping from my face down onto my exposed flesh. I fell into the chair and then with a thud onto the floor, knowing that this was it. He was going to rape me or kill me, or both. All I could think of was that I didn't want Zoey to see me like this.

"If this is how you want it, then this is how you'll get it," he said.

My face was aching, and my ribs and arms were bruised and sore. I knew this was it, one way or the other.

He leaned over me, with his stinking breath in my face. "I love you, and I know you love me."

I couldn't respond. I couldn't move. He was just too strong for me to get away. Tears poured from my eyes as I stared at the wall, avoiding eye contact with him as much as I could. How could this be happening? Here was a man I had once loved, who I thought was dead, now about to change my life one more time. I tensed up in preparation for what was about to happen, still trying to push him off me, when suddenly, I heard a door slam.

"Get off her now, or I'll blow your fucking brains out!"

But Junior didn't move. It was almost as if he didn't hear him. He kept trying to keep my legs apart with his knees, and he held my arms above my head. He seemed oddly unfazed. That's all it took. The sound of the gun blast was almost deafening. Junior's expression changed to confusion as he fell on top of me. Mase ran toward us and pulled Junior's body off mine.

"Mom!"

It was Z calling from her bedroom. We could hear the bedroom door open halfway down the hall.

Mase bolted across the room to intercept her before she saw the bloody scene. He emerged a little while later.

"I told her it was thunder and told her a quick story. She's out like a light."

"Good." I sighed and tried to find the strength to gather my clothes. Mase scooped me off the floor and cradled my body against his chest as he laid me down on the couch and covered my nakedness with a blanket.

Our heartbeats and breathing returned to normal as the intensity of the moment diminished. His face was still flush with color as he stroked my hair, a trace of fear still in his eyes.

"I'm so sorry I didn't get here sooner," he whispered, "everything's going to be okay, I promise," he whispered. He held me tightly and I felt tears swell until I couldn't hold them back anymore. The safety of his arms, his kindness and his love allowed them to flow unconstrained until they were completely purged, and I was completely spent. Mase wiped the streaks on my face with his thumbs before he stood and stepped over Junior's lifeless body. He returned a few minutes later, on the phone and with some ice wrapped in a dish cloth for my face.

****

The police were thoughtfully quiet while I sat numbly watching as my dead husband was carried outside with a sheet over him, again.

"I just have a few more questions," said a deputy I didn't know.

"Okay," I said, but Mase interrupted. "I can answer those. Why don't we give Lanie a moment to gather her thoughts and talk outside?" he offered, and they both headed towards the front door.

The deputy agreed, "okay. I just need the attacker's full name."

Mase responded as he closed the door behind them, "John Robert. . ." and the door shut with a click.

Chapter 16

"Where is he?" I practically bellowed as I flung open their front door and barged into their living room.

"Hi to you, too," Lisa said, and then looked up and made eye contact. "My God, what's wrong, Mel? What happened to your face?"

I started rambling about Junior, Mase, Anonymous…the words were forcing themselves out of my mouth all at the same time and I was incomprehensible.

"Take a minute and catch your breath," she said. "Sit down and tell me what happened."

I sat down and took a long, deep breath.

Ad stepped out of the bathroom with a towel around his waist, toothbrush in hand, and foam in his mouth. I darted toward him and hurled myself into him, hitting his chest with the palms of my hand. He stumbled backwards into the wall and knocked a picture of Buddy to the floor.

"You knew, you bastard! You knew and you didn't tell me!"

The color left his face.

Lisa pulled me back. "What's wrong? Tell me!" she screamed.

Ad composed himself.

"Sit down, Lanie," he said, choking out a whisper, looking weirdly relieved, like he was expecting this conversation, "and I'll tell you everything."

Lisa looked genuinely confused and sat next to me on the couch while I tried to get a grip. I was furious and I could barely contain it.

"What's going on, Adam?" Lisa asked firmly.

The tension was unbearable.

"Yes, please tell us what's going on," I demanded.

"I'll be right back," he said and disappeared into the bathroom, presumably to put on clothes.

"Mel what happened to your face?" She asked, gently touching the scrapes on my cheeks while we waited for Ad's return.

"Junior," I said bluntly.

Ad re-emerged before I could finish, wearing shorts and a worn-out t-shirt. He sat on the chair across from us and appeared to be weighing his words. As he began to speak, Mase materialized in the doorway.

****

After the police left last night, I declined his thoughtful but persistent suggestion to go to the hospital, "just to make sure you're okay" and crawled into bed with Z. I needed to be close to her, to feel our unconditional love. As soon as I slid in next to her, I felt more grounded. I stretched out, laid my head on her pillow, and immediately found myself thinking about Junior calling Ad a "dumbass" and Adam and the senator "pieces of shit." This must have been why Ad had been acting so weird. He had some kind of relationship with Junior. *But how could this be? And how could he hide the fact that Junior was alive?* It was almost impossible to conceive that Adam would have kept something like this from me. And did Lisa know? Surely not, or she wouldn't have us trying to figure out what was going on with him. She would never betray me. And then there was the other revelation that I prayed I misunderstood. Mase told the deputy sheriff that Junior's name was John Robert. I was certain I never told him Junior's real name and I couldn't think of a plausible circumstance where Lisa would tell him. I was overwhelmed by these competing narratives, and I drifted in and out of restless sleep until Zoey awoke. I did my best to seem normal as we dressed, and I lied that I slipped on some ice from the freezer and that is why my face was bruised. We hit the McDonald's drive thru on our way to Ray and Mary Sue's, where to Z's happy surprise Mary Sue had agreed, thankfully without questions at least for the time being, she could spend the day. I made a beeline directly to Lisa's and ignored the call from Mase. I could only handle one thing at a time.

****

Without invitation or saying a word, Mase let himself in and took a seat on the overstuffed chair near the door, to the side of us and across from Adam

"I guess you know," Ad said quietly, "that Junior is alive."

"Was alive," Mase interjected angrily. "I shot him while he was trying to rape Lanie. I wondered what Mase knew about Junior's life in Banjoland, but for the moment that would have to wait.

We all stared at Adam expectantly, needing, waiting, for the details.

"Obviously, he wasn't dead when you shot him in SoHo," Ad said, picking up the narrative. In one breath he explained: "Comatose, but not dead. I told the hospital that they should contact me regarding his progress, that I had your proxy, and when it looked like he was going to recover, Lisa's dad (NY Rep Dennis Marcone) and I decided it would be best for you to avoid being dragged through a difficult and emotional trial, where outcomes are uncertain and for Junior to avoid jail time, for him to be in something like a witness protection program. Basically, he agreed to start a new life to avoid prosecution. He had to take on a new identity and agree never to contact you or Zoey. If he broke his end of the bargain Lisa's father would see to it that he would spend at least twenty-five years in prison."

We took a collective breath, and no one spoke for at least a minute. One by one, they looked at me.

"You decided what was best for me?" I stammered, finding my voice, and trying to absorb the fact that I didn't really kill Junior, that my hunch about him stalking me was correct, and that Ad knew all along.

"What if I wanted him prosecuted?" I shrieked at him. "What if I wanted the process? What if I wanted to make the decisions that affect me and Zoey?" I heard myself shouting at him and I sounded like a wounded little girl.

In one breath and without any filter I proceeded to recount for them the texts and the house thing and how I didn't know if it was Junior or even Ray that could be Anonymous, or what the hell was happening, and how I was worried about Zoey and how I didn't want to stress Lisa while she was pregnant with Ad acting all weird. And all along he knew.

Lisa looked stricken. But she also wasn't stupid.

"You didn't have any idea?" I turned to face her next to me.

"I knew what you knew," she said tersely, but her tone was directed at Adam and not me. "My husband chose not to share with me either." Her disgust was palpable. "I started to really consider the possibility after the McAllister's incident," she said, "but when I mentioned it to Adam, he played it off as ridiculous."

I felt like I was going to vomit, I was so consumed with rage.

Adam filled in the rest of the blanks almost robotically. Basically, Lisa's dad had Junior sent to work for Senator Downes—the senators were college fraternity brothers— and Ad, as his right hand, was supposed to provide oversight.

As if reading my mind, he explained, "The senator has a large operation that includes much more than his legislative duties. He put Junior in charge of receiving rents from various properties as well as made him an integral player in business development."

This made sense. In New York, when he worked for his family, this is exactly what Junior did. He had surprising talent identifying new income opportunities but an even better ability to recognize those that would not succeed. He was easy on the eyes and a consummate gentleman. Anyone who didn't know would completely miss his Jekyll/Hyde business-man persona and the abusive dick he would become behind closed doors.

Lisa's idea for Zoey and me to move to Banjoland was completely unexpected, by any of us, and explained Ad's lack of enthusiasm that day in his kitchen when Z announced that I got the job and we would for certain be permanent residents of Banjoland.

"Obviously things got out of control," his voice fading until he finally stopped talking.

I was relieved that my instincts were right about what was happening in my life, and at the same time I was angrier than I had ever been at anyone other than my dead husband. It felt like I was in the middle of someone else's life, in a novel full of lies and betrayal—the sound of a distant lawn mower was the only thing tying me to reality.

Mase was the first to speak. He had been so quiet I had almost forgotten he was there.

"That was a lot of information—maybe we should just go so you can have some time to think," he said, and reached out offering me his hand as he stood.

I said, "Not so fast."

He looked surprised and sat back down. "What?"

Lisa said, "Oh God, there's more?"

You could hear a pin drop.

I looked Mase directly in the eyes. "Tell me how you knew Junior's name was John Robert."

Please let him have a plausible and reasonable answer. An acceptable answer.

He looked genuinely surprised, and I could see his mind working as he tried to figure out how I might know that he knew this seemingly innocuous detail. Ad slinked back in his chair relieved that the spotlight was off him.

"He was my big case," Mase began. "Only I didn't put together who he was until last week."

Ten minutes later we sat stunned by his revelation.

Chapter 17

"Can you believe it?" Lisa asked. We were sitting on my porch. There was a light morning breeze.

She packed some things and left with me after Ad's revelation, presumably to think and to decide what she wanted to do regarding her marriage and his betrayal. It was nice having her stay with me, despite the circumstances.

"No, it's all just too much."

"It kinda makes sense," she said thoughtfully. "Extortion and racketeering were right up his alley, but drug dealing? That's new."

Mase's bombshell that Junior was involved at some level of criminal activity, was no surprise—his family was involved in lots of different kinds of organized crime in New York—the bombshell, to me, was that he had discovered Junior's identity a week before and chose not to tell me. It didn't interest me at all that Junior was using his position with the senator to gain access to opportunities he wouldn't have otherwise had—he was always an opportunist. Mase explained that once they figured out Junior was the point man it took him more time than he wanted to admit figuring out who Junior really was because Junior was using a different name. This explanation was likely true. It wasn't until he uncovered his name as John Robert, he said, "also known as Junior by some" that he put the pieces together. I didn't pay much attention to the story after that as I was more focused on the fact that he didn't tell me immediately. His justification was plausible, and possibly considerate, even if it was the wrong choice.

"We were about to make an arrest," he'd said, "we were just waiting for him to meet up one last time with our informant, and that was supposed to happen this weekend. We had him under 24/7 surveillance, so I didn't think you were in any danger. When we realized we lost our visual with him I kept calling you, but you didn't answer, and I knew something was wrong. I'm just really glad I got there when I did."

He said a lot in those ten minutes.

"It doesn't surprise me, Leese, I mean we both know who he is. Was. But Mase should have told me. I was looking over my shoulder waiting for the hammer to drop. He let me continue to worry when he could've told me the truth."

I was torn between relief that Junior was dead again, Ad's betrayal to me and to Lisa, and stress for my best friend. Her due date was less than a month away and she had no plan. As far as Mase, I understood his explanation, but I just needed time to myself to breathe and to process all that happened in the span of a couple of months. As for Lisa, all she would say is "I just need time to think," to me and to Ad, who was untiring in his efforts to "make her understand."

He texted, —*I just need to talk to both of you, please. I won't take long. Please*—

It was all I could do not to implode whenever I thought about what happened. We could've avoided everything had Ad just been honest, including, and I didn't think it was over dramatic to describe it this way, my brush with death. I had no doubt whatsoever that Junior could've killed me, and honestly, I wasn't over it. The best course of action, I thought, would be to try to return our lives to some semblance of a routine and create as much normalcy for me and Z as possible. So that is what we did. Lisa would make the right choice for her and while I understood Mase's reasons for not cluing me in right away on Junior, I felt like I needed to take a break from him.

****

It took us, well me, some time to get back into our routine and to just relax. Zoey continued hanging out with RJ and Ray, which was her routine, and I was grateful for it despite the fact that they provided a continual need for explanation.

"How come people in Banjoland kill their own food, Mom?" she asked over a bowl of macaroni and cheese one evening at supper.

"Well, someone's got to do it, I guess," I said. "The land provides."

At this comment she grinned from ear to ear and so did I.

"And how come Mr. Ray says a woman's place is in the kitchen? And why does RJ say girls can't play baseball? I finally just had to tell him to get over himself and girls could do whatever they want."

I enjoyed this age with Z. We could carry on meaningful conversations and enjoy each other's company and I genuinely liked her personality. We were a good match.

"Oh, and Mom, how long is Aunt Leese going to stay with us?" she asked, taking a gulp of milk that left her with a thin white mustache above her lip. "I mean, I like her being here, ya know, but shouldn't she be at her own house with Uncle Adam when the baby comes?"

"Well, I hope she will be," I said, as I envisioned being woken by a crying baby in the middle of the night but sincerely wanting her to make the right choice for her and the baby. As for Ad, I was so angry I didn't care how he felt. "Sometimes adult relationships are a little…complicated," I explained.

"I know, Mom, like you and my dad," she said, shoveling another spoonful of macaroni and cheese into her mouth.

"Yes." I nodded as I poured more milk into her Hello Kitty cup. While I was pondering what to say next, there was a knock at the front door.

"Chop chop, Mom," Zoey said, scrolling through her tablet and taking her last bite of supper, "and you might want to put some clothes on."

I was in my traditional after work look that consisted of boxers and a t-shirt, with my hair in a ponytail on top of my head.

"It's called relaxing, and they *are* clothes," I said on my way to answer the door.

"Hi."

I hadn't seen him since the day of revelation, as Leese and I were now referring to the day in her living room when we found out the truth. He texted daily, more as informational communication, things like "take a look at Merritt's Pond next time you go that way. There's a new boat dock" and to let me know he wasn't going anywhere, but he didn't press to meet or expect a response. And mostly I didn't respond. But I had softened some after having time to think. I knew he loved me and even though I thought he made the wrong choice,

I did understand.

He had flowers in one hand, candy in the other and a goofy, sexy smile on his face. I started to thaw.

"Hi," I answered back.

He dropped the flowers and candy and pulled me close, and I melted into him. He kissed me softly at first and when I responded, his kiss became deeper and urgent.

"Mase!" Zoey ran across the room and jumped into his arms.

"Hey little lady," he picked her up, kissed her cheek and lifted her over his head, then returned her gently to the floor.

"I'm glad you and my mom finally resolved your differences," she said, sounding more like a teenager than a little girl.

"Me too," he said. "Me too."

Zoey scampered off to her room, leaving us alone.

"I have missed you, Lane," he whispered, kissing me slowly. "Isn't it Zoey's bedtime?" he asked with a smirk that let me know exactly what he was thinking. I was thinking the same thing.

Our moment was interrupted by the sound of banjos coming from inside my purse. It was Lisa calling me, upset, from the county jail.

"Calm down, take a breath, and tell me what's going on," I said.

"It's Adam," she said, trying not to sound hysterical, "he's been arrested. They won't tell me why and I can't see him until tomorrow. Can you go with me?"

****

I left work at lunch because that was the scheduled visiting time and met her in town. The county jail was a

nothing I could do to make the situation better for anybody.

Mental Note: When this is over and our lives are at peace, I need to write a book. This was unbelievable.

Chapter 18

Adam had seventy-two hours to decide on the plea deal. Mase was busy working on the "Junior" case that wasn't over and that he said would implicate "big players" that he couldn't discuss and wouldn't even offer a clue as to what else it involved.

"Mase. Was Ad involved *with* Junior in committing those crimes? I thought he was just supposed to *manage* him."

He said lightly, "you know I can't say," kissed my cheek, grabbed his keys and was out the door before I could press him for more information.

****

Billy Joe and Sue Ellen were having one of their many Saturday night gatherings, and I thought it would be a nice distraction for all of us—something to take our minds off the cluster our lives had become once again. Lisa was on her way over to meet Z and me, and we were going into town to get some shrimp from the fish guy to make gumbo for the event they decided would be a low country boil. Given all that happened, I thought she was managing her emotional roller coaster fairly-well by mostly focusing on having the baby.

While we waited for her, Zoey decided that it would be helpful for her Patsy Cline obsession if I helped her make a playlist, and I had no idea Patsy had over 100 songs in her collection. She plopped down on the couch next to me, and handed me her tablet.

"It's all set," she said, "just choose the payment method, hit enter and the download will start."

I laughed, chose the correct payment method, and Patsy entered our world, lock, stock, and barrel.

I handed her back the tablet and swiped my phone, which despite Z's argument, still had the banjo ringtone and not *Crazy* by Patsy.

"Hey sexy lady."

"Hey yourself."

"Lisa's not answering her cell. Is she there by any chance?"

"I knew you had a thing for her," I joked, "but no, she's not here yet."

He chuckled.

"Adam took the deal," he said, "and she needs to come sign some paperwork to bond him out. They said they tried to reach her, but I knew if anyone could, you could."

"Amen," I said, relieved.

"No jail time if he can produce the ledger," he said.

"Mase, you know about the ledger?" I asked.

"I do," he said.

Then I knew. "Did you talk to Adam?" I asked. "Is this part of the case you've been working on?"

"Don't ask me about my business," he said in his best Godfather imitation, and I immediately pictured him saying these words as Michael Corleone.

The big case. Right away I started to put together the pieces of the puzzle, a little disappointed in myself that I hadn't figured it out earlier though in my defense, I had been a bit distracted.

"So," I said, "can you tell me what evidence there is

against him?"

"Not really. If Adam can't produce the ledger with the proof of what he's saying, he'll be fully prosecuted."

The government…Mase…wanted that leather book just as much as the senator did.

"I don't suppose you'd like to tell me what you know," he said.

*What did **he** know? How involved could he be if they were going to prosecute his father?*

"Just what Lisa told me, you know, about the Ledger and the offer to make a deal."

"Hang on a minute, Mase, this might be her beeping in."

"May I speak to Melanie, please?"

"This is she."

"This is Officer Metzger, Clarksville state trooper," he said.

A chill ran through my body.

"I'm sorry to have to call you but you were the last call Lisa made using her cell phone, and we need to reach her family. There's been an accident," he said. "Do you know how we can reach her family?"

Oh my God. Oh my God. Breathe. Breathe.

"Her husband is unreachable at the moment, but I am family," I said, saying a prayer before I continued. "What happened. . . is she okay?"

Please. Please. Please, be okay.

"She's at the hospital and that's all I can tell you," he said.

I hung up before he finished talking. I barely remembered Mase was on the other line.

"That was the police. Lisa's been in an accident." I was speed talking.

"Slow down," he said. "Tell me what happened."

"She's been in an accident and she's at the hospital. I need to go right now."

"Lisa?"

"Yes, Lisa."

I was scared and unintentionally short with him.

"Did they say what happened?" he asked.

"Just that there was an accident and she's at the hospital. Can you come stay with Z so I can go?" I asked, tying my sneakers and grabbing my keys.

"I don't think that's a good idea. We'll all go. I'll come get you. I know you're scared," he said, "but it's going to be all right."

I didn't want to wait for him, but I knew I should. It would take him at least fifteen minutes to get to me and then it would take us at least another fifteen to get to her. I could barely contain my thoughts and thought about leaving Zoey alone for ten minutes until he got here. I fought the urge to leave and made a conscious effort to calm down. I called the hospital, but they couldn't tell me anything more than she'd been brought in about an hour earlier, and I was relieved that they didn't give me very bad news.

"Zoey, put your shoes on and grab your clutch. Aunt Lisa's been in an accident and is at the hospital getting checked out. We're going to see how she's doing."

I did my best to remain calm on the outside.

After pausing for a minute to think about this information, she said, "I'm sure she'll be okay, Mom. No need to fall to pieces." And she walked off proudly humming this Patsy Cline classic, *I Fall to Pieces*.

Mase showed up in record time and we didn't give him a chance to turn off his truck. He barely came to a stop before I snatched door open, tossed Z into the backseat and buckled myself in. I didn't say much.

On our way Zoey and Mase chatted about how boys are always named something "junior." She didn't accept his explanation that girls couldn't be "juniors."

"Girls should be able to be whatever boys can be," she said, seriously.

"I don't make the rules, Zoey," he said.

I appreciated his effort to keep her occupied because I didn't feel like making small talk, and I let their conversation fade into the background as I thought about when Leese and I first met and how much I loved her and how I didn't know what I would do if anything happened to her.

We pulled into the parking lot as close to the Emergency Room as we could and entered the hospital passing sick babies and a boy with a bloody nose, to reach the nurse who seemed to be in charge.

I hovered near the nurse's station, trying to get her attention. "Ma'am? Ma'am? Could you please tell us what is going on with Lisa Marcone? She was brough in about an hour and a half ago."

"And you are?" said the nurse without looking up from her clipboard.

"I am her best friend. Her only family is her husband and he's unavailable."

"Can I please see her?"

"Only family members are allowed . . ."

Tears of frustration were building, and I felt helpless.

Mase interjected, quietly but professionally.

"Excuse me, ma'am," he said, "the only family she has here is her husband, and he's incarcerated at the moment."

He discreetly showed his badge and continued, "My gal here is the next closest thing that your patient has to family, and I assure you, she would want to see her."

"Hang on," the nurse said gruffly, and snatched her clipboard, disappearing behind large double doors into the patient care area.

Zoey watched in silence.

Eventually she returned with instructions that I would have to talk with the doctor first and then I could see Lisa.

"Okay, thank you," I said gratefully. We made our way to the waiting area and sat as far away from the gaggle of sneezing, coughing children and their harried parents and the others with their unknown ailments as we could.

By that time, Ray and Mary Sue had arrived, along with others. They had no idea what happened, but word in Banjoland travels fast.

"There's been an accident," I explained. "They brought Lisa in, but no one's told me anything yet. I'm waiting for the doctor."

We stood together in awkward silence, not knowing what to say.

The doctor finally emerged from behind the double doors. He called my name and motioned to me. I approached him apprehensively.

"I'm sorry, ma'am, but your friend was involved in a car accident, and . . ." he looked down at his records to make sure he got the name right, "Lisa, well she's in bad shape and it doesn't look good."

Part of me wondered how many times he had to say this to strangers and if he had become immune to the impact of the words he was delivering. He was so matter-of-fact as he told me that my best friend—the one person I could totally trust, the person besides my daughter that I loved the most in the world—might not make it.

"And the baby,?" I asked quietly.

"He was delivered through c-section when they first arrived. It's touch and go with babies born out of trauma, as you might imagine," he said, "but he's got a good chance since he was fully developed."

"Can I see her, please?"

"You can, but I need to remind you that she's in bad shape."

*Bad shape...she's in bad shape...She's . . .*I stopped myself.

I turned to Mase, who was standing directly behind me.

"Would you like me to come with you?" he offered.

His genuine look of concern touched me.

"No, thank you, though. I'd like to do this alone."

I followed the doctor back to the bay where Lisa was being treated. I slowly pulled back the curtain and stepped inside. I wasn't afraid of what I might see. I needed to see. I pulled up a chair and sat down next to her. She was almost as white as the blanket that was covering her body. The room was cold and quiet except for the humming of machines and an occasional beep from a random monitor.

"What the hell?" I whispered, "You can't leave me alone in Banjoland." I took her hand from under the blanket and held it against my cheek. I began to sob softly.

"I love you so much. You can't die"

Okay, Lanie, get a grip. I wiped my tears, inhaled

deeply, and took inventory of what I saw.

Lisa had tubes down her throat and her lips were purple and cut and bruised. Part of her head looked dented in and big patches of sticky blood matted her beautiful hair. Her eyes were closed, but one side was black and blue. She had a deep cut on the side of her neck that had several wide stiches in it. I wondered if she was white like that because of all the blood she'd lost. She was in a coma and despite her injuries, she looked peaceful.

I hadn't been through anything like this since Sissy died. At least Leese was still alive, and that meant there was hope.

"I told you I couldn't take another person I love dying," I chastised her. "I just love you so much." I kissed her cold hand as I held it between both of mine, her fingernails still sporting the pea green polish she and Z had chosen on our most recent shopping adventure. I thought about the years of support and encouragement, the love and acceptance that she had given me.

Because of the placement of the sheet and blanket across her body, it was obvious that the baby was no longer inside her. I wondered where he was.

The doctor poked his head inside the curtain. "Ma'am, you're going to have to leave soon."

"Okay." I nodded, resenting his intrusion. "Well, my sweet, sweet Leese, they're trying to move me out."

I didn't want to leave. What if something happened and I wasn't here?

"I don't know what I would do without you," I said. "Don't you leave me now."

I stood up and slid my chair back against the wall. I leaned over and rubbed my cheek against hers. "I love you, Lisa Marie Marcone." I reached over and pushed her hair back from her face and kissed her cold and bruised cheek.

"I mean it, don't you leave me."

The tears started again, but I knew my hospital visit wasn't over.

"Excuse me…ma'am, where's her baby?" I asked someone, a nurse or an orderly I suppose, who walked by as I pointed toward Lisa's bay.

She pointed to the double doors near the end of the hall.

"He's in ICU, through those doors."

I wandered down the hall and through the doors to the nurse's station.

"Um," I whispered, barely able to speak, "my friend was just brought in because she was in a car accident. Her son is in pediatric ICU. Can I please see him?"

The nurse just assumed, I guess, that it was okay for me to be there and pointed across the hall and to the right from where we were, to room four.

I nodded a thank you and slowly, cautiously, entered the room. There were machines and monitors making all kinds of sounds, some with blinking lights and numbers, and there were rocking chairs and cribs for several babies. But only one baby was in there. Our baby. He looked peaceful, even with all the tubes and machines hooked up to him. He seemed to be normal size with a mop of black hair and a nose just like Lisa's.

I spontaneously broke out into tears.

A nurse came in, looked at him, read the monitors and made some notes.

"Would you like to hold him?" she asked.

"Can I?" I responded, surprised.

She went on to explain that it was good for babies to be held, that everyone needed to experience human touch.

"Is he...will he be okay?" I asked.

"I think so," she said. "Because his birth was caused by trauma, we need to observe him and make sure all his functions are normal. He's quite well developed, though, and that's a very good sign."

I thought about all the donuts Lisa had eaten.

He wasn't in one of those plastic, sterile, covered cribs. His was open and the nurse unfastened something so I could hold him without getting caught in any tubing or cords. She reached in and gently lifted his little body and handed him into my outstretched arms.

His face wasn't scrunched and his head wasn't pointed like Zoey's was when she was born. I'm sure that was because they had to do the c-section.

I was very careful with him. He looked perfect. Well, aside from a few cuts along his right cheek.

"Oh, little man," I whispered to him, "you are so loved."

I held his little body tightly against my chest. The last time I touched him he was still inside his mommy's tummy. More tears came. Would Leese ever get to see him, hold him and breathe him in? How could it be that I was the first of us to do all this? I was completely overwhelmed. At the nurse's prompt I handed him back, but not before inhaling his smell one more time and nuzzling his cheek with mine.

I walked aimlessly back toward the lobby with random thoughts racing through my mind. I was struggling to wake up from this nightmare. Sue Ellen handed me a tissue and our friends surrounded me, waiting for me to finish blowing my nose and give them details.

"Lisa's in bad shape," I reported, detached, same as the doctor.

"We know, honey," Mase said. He pulled me close to him.

It was like we were alone in the room, even though there were people all around us with their own emergencies.

"Does anyone know what happened?" I coughed out, blowing my nose with the damp tissue.

"According to the police," Mase said quietly, "someone forced her off the road."

"Forced her off the road?"

"I spoke with Officer Metzger, the state trooper, and he said they have reason to believe she was run off the road, but I don't have the details yet. They're following up on leads right now."

I sighed deeply and let him absorb me into his hug. None of this made any sense at all, and I still had one more thing to do before we left.

"Babe, I need to chat with you for a minute," I said, as I walked toward where Zoey and RJ were playing.

She didn't respond.

"Zoey," I said, a little bit louder.

She looked up at me, and I held out my arms to pick her up, even though she had long been too big for that.

I tried to hold back my tears. "Zoey . . ." I wanted her to think I was strong, that I could handle anything, so I always tried to hide unpleasant emotions from her. I never wanted her to be afraid. It was my job to protect her. This time it was all I could do not to break down and start sobbing.

She put her little hands on my cheeks and tried to wipe my tears away. "It's okay, Mom."

"Z, Aunt Lisa got hurt pretty badly in the car accident."

As I said these words, I did begin to weep. I didn't want to come unglued but I couldn't help it. I was engulfed by genuine worry.

Mase chipped in. "Do you understand what your mom is saying, sweetie?" He was kneeling on one knee and holding her soft, painted hands in his.

"Yes, I understand. I'm not a baby," she said. "It's okay, Mom." She put her arms around my neck and continued. "Remember what the Reverend Jeremiah P Johnson of the White Oak Primitive Fundamental Baptist Church said on TV the other day?"

I spontaneously laughed out loud at this.

"Remember he said that we live forever, that we never die, sometimes we just move to a different neighborhood? If Aunt Lisa moves to another neighborhood, one day we'll move to that place, too," she said and added, "you know, if she's saved. And I'm sure she is because Aunt Leese saved a lot. Remember? She always said, 'save before you spend.'"

What could I say after that? She seemed okay, like everything made sense.

Chapter 19

The guard left us alone in a small dingy room furnished with a gray metal table and three folding chairs. A green metal light fixture with one naked light bulb in it hung by a wire over the table. It looked like an interrogation room from any TV law series. There was a bottle of water on the table in front of each chair. We stood and hugged each other under the supervision of a guard. He looked terribly disheveled and tired. I was torn between anger for what he withheld from me and for what he had done to his family, and pity for his current circumstances, Lisa's accident included. I was determined to take the higher road, for Lisa's sake and put my anger at his betrayal on the back burner.

"I know it's a ridiculous question," I said, "but how are you? Is there anything you need from me?"

"Well," he began, barely audible, when we were interrupted by his attorney.

"Thanks for coming, Melanie," the attorney said, holding his hand out toward me. "My name is Michael DeMarco and I am representing Adam."

"Nice to meet you." I reached across the table to shake his hand.

"Thanks again for coming. I know this is a very difficult time for everyone, but there are some extremely important issues that we need to discuss."

Ad stared blankly at me.

"Okay," I said, a little apprehensively.

He opened his briefcase and took out a yellow pad and a pen. "Do you mind if I take notes?"

"I guess not," I said.

"As I'm sure you know, Adam wants to make a plea deal that revolves around the information contained in Senator Downes' ledger.

I nodded in the affirmative.

"Before we go any further, we need your assurance that what we discuss is between us and that you won't share it with anyone, especially Mason Downes."

Even in my dulled state I knew what this meant. Adam would have to go to trial if he didn't have the proof he needed to make the deal, and Mase was on the other side—the government, aka prosecution's side and have to give them all of the information he had about anything related to the case.

I took a long drink of tepid water from the bottle in front of me. I loved Mase, and he was an investigator, not a lawyer, so this didn't initially seem like a big deal. He kept his business separate from his relationship with me, and I couldn't foresee any problems between us if I did the same.

"Okay," I agreed. This shouldn't be a big deal—Ad just needed to turn over the ledger.

"Great," DeMarco said. "Here's where we stand now. Lisa was bringing me the ledger—she was supposed to drop it off—on her way to your house when she was run off the road. The problem is that the investigators said they didn't find it in her car or on the scene anywhere."

The glare from the single light bulb was distracting as it cast deformed shadows on the dirty wall behind him.

I took another drink of water from the bottle, splashed a little on my face, and pondered this new information.

"I'm not sure what this has to do with me, Mr. DeMarco," I said, connecting the dots.

I looked across at Ad who sat stone-faced with his hands folded on the table. His bloodshot eyes were swollen.

"Well," he paused, "we need your help."

Ad spoke for the first time.

"I don't mean to pressure you, Lanie," he said, "but you're the only one I can trust. I know after everything I have no right to ask you, but you're the only one that can help."

I finished my water. It felt like I was under the hot lights of an interrogation myself.

"Okay." I would do whatever I could to help Ad, and I would do it for my sweet Leese.

A slight smile briefly crossed Ad's face.

Then Michael DeMarco said, "Okay, that's a start." He jotted some notes on his pad.

"What do I need to do?"

"We need you to find out what Mason knows, and what they have against Adam. They will eventually have to turn everything over to us, but we don't need any surprises and we need to be as prepared as possible."

I immediately felt guilty and realized that was ridiculous because I hadn't done anything, but even having a conversation about this made me feel disloyal to Mase.

"You want me to be a spy?" I asked, throwing Ad a doubtful glance.

"Well…I wouldn't put it like that," DeMarco said.

It was one thing for me not to share information

about Ad and his case with Mason, but to actively deceive him and betray his trust was something I was not prepared to do. And now I had more questions.

"Are you saying that someone from the government ran her off the road?"

Before he could answer, I figured it out.

"Oh I get it. You think whoever investigated the scene might have the ledger," I said.

"Yes," Mike DeMarco said.

"Well don't the prosecutors have to tell you what evidence they have against Adam?" I asked, recalling the procedures from all the TV law I watched over the years.

"They do, but they can hold on to it until right before trial if they choose, and frankly, we don't need any to have any more unforeseen issues to deal with."

"What about the person that ran her off the road?" I asked. "Who do you think it is?"

"We have our ideas about that," he said, clearly not wanting to discuss what those ideas were. "We need to wait for the forensics to come in."

Now I was asking the questions.

"What does this ledger look like?" I asked.

Ad spoke up.

"Well, it is black and leather bound, about a couple hundred pages or so, and it was filled with names, dollar amounts, and each dollar amount had a corresponding description to identify what the money was to be used for."

DeMarco jotted on his notepad.

"No wonder the senator is having a meltdown, but Ad," I said, "how was Junior involved in all of this?"

He glanced across the table at DeMarco, who nodded as permission for him to continue.

165

"It is a long story, Lanie, and I'll spare you all the details, but Junior started out as kind of a '"do whatever needs to be done'" guy and then he began doing what he does, and the senator was impressed with his ability to '"identify opportunities"' as he explained it to me." He took a drink of water from the sweaty bottle on the table and continued, "and so he gave him more responsibility and authority and Junior became harder and harder to control. I tried to explain to him the kind of man Junior is. Was. But he didn't listen and began to treat him like more of a colleague than an employee. Needless to say, things finally hit the fan."

He looked apologetic, almost pained as he spoke. When he was finished, I sat quietly for a few minutes while I absorbed this information.

Mike DeMarco made a few more notes and then set the pen and pad on the table, took off his Gucci glasses and set them on the pad and ran his fingers through his product-filled hair. He didn't speak while he quietly pondered what it was that lawyers thought about.

As I stood to leave, assuming I was finished with this unpleasantness, Michael DeMarco said, "There's one more thing, Melanie."

I waited.

"There is the matter of AJ."

"Excuse me?" I sat back down.

Adam spoke up and cleared his throat. "Lanie, I know this is a lot to ask, but I'm not sure how long I will be here and what's going to happen with all of this and with...Lisa . . ." he choked up a little, "but I...I need someone to keep AJ for me until I can get out of here for good."

His eyes were pleading.

I nodded. "Don't give it another thought. Of course I'll take care of him."

He produced a tiny smile and looked relieved while DeMarco slid paperwork in front of me.

"These just give you temporary legal rights with regard to the minor child," he said. "Sign here…here…and here."

In retrospect I should have considered what Mase might have to say about this, but I didn't, I just acted. I loved him, though, and hoped he would understand. He would, just as I understood why he resisted sharing his work information with me. You can't really investigate government corruption and lay all your cards on the table. Still, I needed to find a way, for Lisa's sake, to help Ad. After thinking about this for less than a minute, I knew exactly what I needed to do.

Chapter 20

He kissed me slowly and tenderly, just like he always did when he had something specific on his mind. He knew just the right way to touch me and I responded almost reflexively. It was like I had no control over my body at all. Our chemistry was undeniable and passionate. I positioned myself on his lap in the middle of the couch and kissed him playfully. Within seconds he was groaning and unhooking my bra.

His fingers slid over my hot skin until they softly, and then more firmly massaged my breasts. The ache between my legs grew with every squeeze and I felt his readiness pushing through his pants. I opened my eyes while we were kissing, because watching his eagerness and the way he was almost devouring me was incredibly sexy. He slid his fingers into my panties and I lifted myself off his lap so he could slide them off. At the same time I was grappling for his buckle and pulled down his zipper. My heart was pounding in anticipation of what I knew was coming. I could not control myself and hearing him groan put me over the edge. We were writhing together and moaning until we finished together. I lifted myself off him, and we collapsed onto the floor next to each other.

"That was great," he said, still breathing heavily and reaching out to take my hand in his.

I nodded in agreement and held his hand, still

catching my breath. I needed that. I needed him—to feel our connection. I was so emotional with everything happening all round me.

"Lanie?"

"Hmm?" I rolled on my side to face him.

"Adam is in some serious trouble," he said, "and I want you to be prepared."

"Prepared for what?" Why did he always choose times like this to discuss heavy subjects?

"If he can't make a deal, he could very likely go to prison for a long time." He continued, "I also want you to know that I see us as endgame. And what that means to me is that we should be able to trust each other."

"Um, endgame?" I asked.

"Yes. Endgame. It means that I see our future together...don't you?"

I did but we hadn't spoken about it so directly before.

"Why Mason Downes," I said in my best Southern accent, "that's so romantic."

He laughed, "I'll do better eventually," he promised, "so?"

"Well, I'll admit I've thought about it," I said, more seriously, glad to finally hear him say it out loud.

He leaned in to kiss me, as if to mark the moment.

"Well then, we have to discuss the Adam situation as honestly as we can," he said, pulling away from me.

I liked that he wanted us to be honest with each other and clear the air. A win for me would be if he just simply told me what he knew about the ledger—no strings attached. I chuckled to myself at how unlikely that scenario would be, but I pressed on anyway.

"I agree," I said, gently running his chest hairs

through my fingers.

His move.

"As you already know, the government is building a corruption case against my father. Adam is small potatoes and really only a means to get my dad."

I nodded to indicate I understood, but this was new information for me. I wondered when all of this came to light if the senator was involved in the corruption and if they were investigating him as well. That made sense.

"The night that we stopped at Redneck Central on our way back from meeting my parents at the club, the envelope I handed Pat was marked money to give to Adam, knowing he would give it to my dad," he said.

My move.

"I'm not sure what you want me to say, Mase," I replied.

"Yes you are," he said. "Tell me what you know about the ledger."

Did this mean that his people didn't have it either?

I was silent for a few minutes.

"Well, we know Ad needs it to make the deal, right?" I asked.

He nodded.

Well…if Ad wasn't really their target and it was Senator Downes, maybe Mase and I could be on the same side here. I was relieved and motivated.

"But if he can't make the deal because he doesn't have it," Mase continued, fidgeting with his zipper, "he will have to testify against my father, and it becomes a 'he said/she said' pile of accusations and mudslinging. The ledger is the only way I can see for him to save himself."

No wonder Ad was an emotional basket case. The

ledger was the nail in the coffin the government needed for what they anticipated would be an open and shut case of bribery, conspiracy, and extortion, among other charges. If Adam didn't have it, everyone assumed the government did or the senator had somehow gotten it back. If the ledger was in the senator's possession the case against him became much more circumstantial. Still convictable, Mase thought, but not nearly as easily.

There was one more thing.

"I get it," I said, "but—"

"I'm out. Once evidence started pointing to my father, they reassigned me. I guess that's good, I don't want to compromise the case or anything."

He slipped on his boxers, headed for the kitchen, and that was the end of our discussion.

Chapter 21

What a difference a month could make. AJ's doctors said he was out of the woods and so I brought him to his hopefully temporary home with us, and Lisa was breathing on her own. She wasn't conscious, but the doctors saw this as a sign that she was healing. I felt a little guilty on the drive home with our community baby for not consulting Mase before I agreed to keep him, because we were a couple and we were end game, I thought with a smile, and things like this were the things couples talked about. But like he said, what other choice did I have? He was supportive and positive and helpful, and I began to realize I couldn't imagine my life without him in it. I was also very fortunate that my boss, Mr. Peel, was aware of our situation and allowed me to work from home. He was so kind to offer me maternity leave, but I just didn't feel right about that, so working from home was our compromise.

"I'll let you show your thankfulness when I get back later," Mase said, after he helped me unload what seemed like the entire baby section from Target—bought to make do and in no way compared to the designer set-up Lisa had ready in his official nursery (minus the senator's gift of antlers).

"You know I will," I said, grabbing his tush as he bent over to grab the last box of diapers, grateful for him.

"Mom, Mom! I want to hold him!" Z chirped,

circling us with her hands wrapped around his diaper bag which she held to her chest in a bear hug, her feet dancing dangerously around the straps.

"Let's get everything in the house and settle for a minute and then of course you can hold him."

"Okay, good, ya know 'cause I need to get some practice for when you and Mase have a baby. They require a lot."

I don't know which surprised me more, her use of the word require, or the thought of having a baby with Mase.

****

Adam was still in jail pending his trial because Mike DeMarco had not been able to work out another plea deal without the ledger. The notoriety of the case kept him from getting bail set, "for his own protection," the federal prosecutor had said.

"What do they mean 'for his own protection,'" I asked Mase, who was looking paternal while he burped AJ.

"It means that they recognize my father is a dangerous man and has a history of making his problems disappear," he explained, matter of fact, like it was business as usual and common knowledge. His lack of emotion where his father was concerned surprised me.

****

I didn't want to go, but Mase said it was important to keep up appearances, and that I couldn't act any differently than I did before our conversation about his father and the case the government was building against him. I was on the inside, now—in the know, and I liked how that felt.

The procedure was the same as before, only this

time no one stopped us at the gate. Mase shared some banter with Simon as he held the door open for Zoey and me, with AJ in my arms.

"Your mom never cooks?" I asked.

"Please. No. We've had every holiday meal here since I was…well, since after West died," he said, "besides she can't be seen if she's at home." That was only the second time I heard him mention his brother's name. It is a Southern thing to name your children with parts or combinations of their parents' names Mase informed me, and since Mase was Mason Westhoven Downes IV, his brother was Ashley (great grandfather) Westhoven "West" Downes. This was unusual to me, but I liked the thought involved and how their heritage continued through the generations.

We followed a path through the tables decorated with a cornucopia or paper turkey, some had pumpkins, toward his family's table. The scene was familiar with minions and wannabes circling, waiting for the next word or command uttered from Olivia's lips. As we approached with our baby gear, people reluctantly moved out of the way.

Everyone exchanged formal greetings and I saw the senator at the bar.

"This is AJ, Mrs. Downes" Zoey introduced in grown up fashion. "He lives with us now 'cause his mom is in the hospital."

"Yes, I've heard," she said, sipping from her martini.

I set AJ in his carrier and motioned for a waiter so I could order a drink.

"Do you really think that's a good idea?" Olivia asked, using a most polite condescending tone. "You do have a baby with you."

"Mother, please," Mase interjected. "Lanie is an adult and perfectly capable of deciding when and where she can have a drink."

I took a long sip of the top shelf champagne and melted into my chair. I had forgotten what it was like to have a newborn, and despite the fact that I was tired and a little cranky I had developed some sympathy for Olivia after Mase's description of her marriage, no thanks to her, and so I ignored her snide comments.

"The club is really not the place for an infant anyway," Olivia mused. She held her hand up ever so slightly when a minion appeared to remove her glass and replace it with a fresh one.

"Pumpkin! Zucchini! A squash!" Zoey was busy naming the contents of the cornucopia centerpiece for Mase as he held up each item. Olivia, uninterested, rose from the table as she lit her cigarette and mingled with the crowd. I finished my drink and as soon as I set the empty glass on the table, Senator Downes appeared with a drink in each hand, one for him and one for me.

"Mind if I sit here?" he asked. He set a drink in front of me. "I thought you might be ready for another one." He was cordial and chatty.

"I am," I said. "Thank you."

I felt dirty just being in his presence.

"Listen," he said, "I'm sorry about your friend and I want you to know I'm doing everything I can to help Adam."

"Lisa," I said, trying to disguise my disgust at having to interact with the man I was sure was responsible for her accident in some way. "Her name is Lisa."

"Yes, Lisa. Is this their son?" He looked at the carrier on the floor next to Mase.

"Yes."

"Can I hold him?" he asked, ever the politician.

"I'd rather you didn't," I answered politely. "He's just fallen asleep, and well, sometimes it's difficult to get him to stay that way."

Give me the academy award. Or him. We both played our roles superbly.

"I understand," he said. He reached behind me to tap on Mason's shoulder. "Hey, son, you can't hog all the beautiful ladies at the table," he said, motioning for Zoey to come sit on his lap.

"Hi, Mr. D," she said and climbed into his lap. "How are things?"

"Things are fine, little lady. I like that nail polish you're wearing."

"Me too. It's called Gaga Green. You know, like Lady Gaga. Me and my Aunt Leese picked it out before she got in the hospital. I need some filler."

"Well, it's a very nice color for you," he said. "It matches your hair nicely."

The lights dimmed, which we knew was the sign that dinner was ready to be served. As the mass began taking their seats, Pat appeared at our table with a security guard standing next to him.

"Excuse me, Senator," the guard said, "but this man insists he is here at your request. We didn't see his name on the approved visitor's list."

The senator looked up from his phone and seemed confused for a moment. Pat was completely out of place here. There were only white people in the club except for the staff, or Help, as Olivia called them, and it was just one more reason for me to avoid coming here.

Mental Note: The club has official security. I wonder why.

"Uh, yes, yes, he is here at my request. I'm sorry for the oversight, Ryan."

"Very well, Senator," Ryan said looking confused—but not as confused as Olivia. He apologized to Pat for the misunderstanding and disappeared into the dimness.

Senator Downes stood up to shake Pat's hand. "Sorry for the oversight. I'm glad you could make it."

Pat simply nodded and took a seat next to Olivia, who looked mortified. It was amusing to see her not in control and a bit flustered. She nodded ever so slightly in Pat's direction but didn't speak when he greeted her, and her unspoken communication with Senator Downes was so unmistakable I think everyone at the table could feel it.

I waved across the table and smiled to acknowledge Pat, and Mase shook his hand as waiters appeared from the fringes, each holding a tray with a complete Thanksgiving dinner on it, including a turkey, and a small pig with an apple in its mouth.

"Mom, Mom, look," Zoey whispered, pointing at the pig. "Are we going to eat that pig's face?"

"Well, not me. I'm taking AJ outside to feed him," I said. "You stay here with Mase and help yourself to some pig face," I smiled and kissed her cheek on my way out.

Mental Note: The Club sucks. It's antiquated and out of touch.

****

"You were very good tonight," Mase said, squeezing my hand.

"It was harder than I thought it'd be."

"You'll get better with practice," he said. "Take it from someone who has experience."

"Mase," I said, softly, when did you realize that your dad was...how he is?"

There was no surprise or aha moment in my own life. I'd known since I was a small child who my father was—I wondered when Mase discovered that his father wasn't the man he thought he was.

"It wasn't just one thing, it was a series of things. It began with an awareness that people acted a certain way around him—with a level of respect that I didn't understand and that I didn't realize until later was really fear. People were eager to do things for him, and consequently, for me. I guess I finally realized he wasn't like other fathers when I was in high school and a friend joked to someone that they better be careful not to cross me because my dad was like the Godfather."

I imagined a long line of people waiting for an audience and to kiss his ring.

"Anyway, as I got older, I saw things and figured out some of what he was doing, but I think what put me over the edge was the women. He had women all over the place and saw them without discretion, and well, you can see what that's done to my mother."

I felt pity for her, and it did explain her need to be the center of attention. It still didn't explain the episode with Sunglasses, at least not in my mind. I'd have to devote a little more thought to that when I had the time. Right now I had too many other priorities. Mase stopped at Redneck Central, which was customary on these trips, to get a beer and a drink for Z if she woke up. She was strapped in the backseat with a regular seatbelt, snuggled with her blanket and lightly snoring. She had kicked off her flats, which was something she'd begun to do wherever we went, as long as her toenails were done. On the other side of the backseat was AJ. He was facing backwards in his car seat and sleeping peacefully. I knew it wouldn't be long before he was awake and hungry. I wondered sentimentally how long we would have him and how my life was so different than it had been even a year ago. Lisa did seem to be getting better. At least that is how I chose to interpret things.

Mase returned and snuffed out his cigarette butt with his shoe before he opened the door. He held out a beer for me.

"No, I'm good," I said, "unless you want baby duty."

"You do for me and I'll do for you," he grinned.

"Why was Pat at the club?" I asked, squeezing his hand but changing the subject. "Didn't that seem weird to you?"

"Yes. I mean obviously it was weird. My father was making a point to be seen in public with him. After you left and we had the pig-face incident—don't ask—my father took him to the bar with a group of his buddies and they all smoked cigars and had drinks. I don't think Pat spoke one word."

"I wonder why Pat showed up. What was in it for him?"

"I don't know," Mase said, "but he's not stupid like my father thinks he is."

We pulled into the driveway just as AJ began to cry. Perfect timing—at least we were home. Mase came around to open my door like he always does, but then stopped and motioned for me to wait a minute. AJ was having none of it, started screaming, and woke up Zoey.

"Mom! Make him stop, he's hurting my ears," she whined.

"Hang on, sweet baby, Aunt Mellie's got you," I said as I leaned over the backseat and unbuckled him. He stopped crying for a moment, but as soon as he realized I didn't have the bottle in my hand he began wailing.

"Mom! Stop him!"

With my left hand I fumbled around for the diaper bag, which was behind my seat in front of Zoey, while I held AJ with my right arm. He was randomly sucking the air, crying, and searching for the nipple. I found the bottle, popped the top off as quickly as I could, and shoved it into his mouth. Zoey had pulled her blanket over her head and wasn't moving.

Grateful for the momentary reprieve, I opened his truck door myself. The night air felt good and I was ready to take a shower and relax. Mase met me on the porch with a bag that had some clothes and toiletries in it.

"What are you doing?" I asked, "I need you to please get Z and bring her in for me."

"Lanie, we need to stay at my house tonight…your house is trashed."

"What?"

"I've called my people and they're on the way. You need to take the truck and go to my house. Now."

I stood there like I didn't understand what he was saying. AJ had finished his bottle and I was holding him against my shoulder and gently patting his back.

"What are you talking about? Let me take a look."

He blocked me from the door in almost the same way he had done with Lisa that night at her house

"Just please do this for me," he said. "I don't want

you upset, and the kids need to go to bed. Trust me, I'll give you the details as soon as we do a once over. Please."

His attempt to keep me out was futile, as I'm sure he expected.

"I just need to take a look."

I brushed past him, handed off AJ and walked through my front door the same way I always did. He was right; it was trashed. Things were broken and torn exactly like they were at Lisa's house. This was serious déjà vu.

I stood paralyzed as I surveyed the damage.

"Mase, why?" I choked out. Junior was dead and I thought we could rest easily. It was too much. Lisa was in a coma, AJ might never know her, Ad was in jail and now my house was trashed. Mase held me and stroked my hair gently while I quietly sobbed until it turned into a full ugly cry.

"I'll know more once we have a chance to look things over," he said leading me outside to his truck, "but I think it's obvious whoever did this thinks you have the ledger, or you know where it is. Now get in the truck and take the kids to my house."

He kissed me on the forehead, strapped AJ in his seat, and shut my door.

"I won't be long," he said, "and don't worry. I'll take care of everything."

Mental Note: I don't want to live this life, I just want some peace. I feel overwhelmed and exhausted and I'm afraid Lisa is going to die. Maybe I really should just go home to SoHo.

Chapter 22

Mason got home after I took a shower and put the kids to bed. After contemplating everything I knew about Ad's situation, and granted, it certainly wasn't a lot, the only theory I had was that Senator Downes still didn't have the ledger so he had his thugs ransack my house because he thought Lisa might have given it to me.

"Right," Mason said, brushing his teeth. He swished, spit and slid into bed next to me. He leaned up against the headboard with his hands crossed behind his head.

"What are we missing?" I asked.

"I'm not sure. Smitty (his work partner) said they are on an all-out hunt for it."

Mason understood why he could not be involved in the investigation anymore, but understanding didn't make it easy. He was restless and bored with the mundane cases they gave him.

At that moment I flashed back to Buddy hanging from a tree and was glad I didn't have a dog.

"What now?" I wondered aloud. "They almost killed Lisa," I added softly and rested my head on his bare chest. "I'm not sure being your girlfriend guarantees me any protection," my words drifted away as I pondered to myself whether I should give up my hopes of being his wife and having his baby and return to home to SoHo.

"You'll always be safe with me," he said and kissed

the top of my head.

I drifted off unsure of anything except our love.

****

Adam and the senator were to go on trial in less than a month, and the key piece of evidence against the senator was still missing. They had other evidence, though, and Mike DeMarco thought it was good circumstantial evidence against both Ad and Senator Downes, but he also thought the senator could easily blame Ad, or the fact that Ad was involved could give the senator plausible deniability. If things didn't work out just right, Ad could be the scapegoat and take the fall for everything. Neither Mase nor I wanted that.

Mase's ringing cell phone halted our breakfast conversation. It was early for someone to be calling, but he answered once he saw who it was.

"Downes here," he said. "Yes. Yes. When?…Okay, thanks." He hung up then said, "That was the Smitty," and set the phone on the table. "Sunglasses is dead."

He looked perplexed and began rubbing his hand through his hair like his brain was on full throttle trying to make sense of everything. The only person I knew to go to who might could help was Ad, and since visitation was on Sunday I would be prepared with questions. The pressure to figure this out was mounting quickly.

****

Ad was looking a bit better than he had immediately after Lisa's accident. He wasn't coifed with product or wearing his designer apparel, but he was clean and neat, and his eyes were not as bloodshot or tired looking as they had been then either.

"There's my boy," he said as he took AJ from my arms and smothered his face into the baby's cheeks and hair and inhaled deeply. "He's gotten so much bigger since last week."

I knew these visits were what was keeping him going. These and the hope that Lisa would be okay and this nightmare would be over one way or another in less than a month.

"Listen, Ad," I said, trying to get comfortable on the metal chair. "Sunglasses is dead."

He took a bottle out of the diaper bag, flipped off the top like a pro, and gave it to AJ, who was starting to get a little fussy, and sat down in the chair next to mine.

He mulled this over for a minute.

"Do they know what happened?"

"He was shot in the chest, and when they found him in a hayfield off of County Road 2, he had duct tape across his mouth and eyes," I reported.

Ad's eyes got big.

"What?" I quizzed.

He explained, "There was a guy that worked for the senator several years ago—before my time. Word has it that he turned on the senator or double-crossed him in some land deal. The next thing they knew, he was found in the middle of a pasture with a gunshot wound to his chest and duct tape across his mouth and eyes."

We sat quietly for a few minutes.

"Ad," I said, "how was Sunglasses involved with Senator Downes?"

"What do you mean?" he asked, lifting AJ to his chest and patting his back.

"I mean what was their relationship?"

This was a pure guess on my part. The only thing I knew about Sunglasses was that he lived on the reservation and that he'd gotten into a tussle with Ad at the shotgun wedding at the Cadillac. Oh, and Lisa's recounting of his interlude with Olivia.

"He is a flunkie," Ad said, "did dirty work—things no one else wanted to get their hands dirty doing...I guess I'm not surprised."

"Because?" I asked.

"Because he played both sides of the fence. He acted like he hated the senator, and really I think he did. But the lure of the money was too much for him to stick by his truth.

"Ad—"

"Yes. I thought about him being the one that ran Lisa off the road. He's done worse," he interrupted, reading my thoughts.

This was an interesting conversation, but we still weren't any closer to getting the ledger. We felt like there should be clues from the investigation of Lisa's accident, but the state forensics lab was so backed up that it took over a month to process a crime scene and get the results back. We knew their report would be in any day. The trial date was coming fast and Adam's freedom was hanging in the balance.

I got up to leave and Ad handed me back his sleeping baby.

"Lanie, I can't thank you enough for taking care of my boy," he said, and smiled genuinely at me. "I wish I had been different with Lisa," he said gently, his eyes moistening as he stared at their child. "I know I should've been honest with her. We were a team. I thought I had it figured out and I didn't want to add any stress to her life."

I didn't say anything.

"And, Lane," he added, "I'm sorry I hurt you, too.

I'm sorry about everything."

He was obviously struggling with his guilt, and honestly, I agreed with him. He should have trusted Lisa; she was his biggest supporter, and he should have told me the truth about Junior, especially after the Flannigans debacle.

"She had faith in you, Ad. Don't get me wrong, she knew something was obviously going on, but she always knew you would work it out," I said. "And I'll forgive you one day."

"Thanks for that, Lanie Lou," he said softly. He gave AJ a tender kiss before we left.

****

"What do you think she wants to talk about?" Mason asked, as we loaded up the children and our necessities.

"I don't really know," I said.

I hadn't been home from visiting Adam that long when I got her message. I couldn't imagine what she would want to talk to me about that would require a visit and not a text.

I thought about my conversations with Mary Sue, usually about the children or our men, or current Banjoland activities. I got the sense that deep down she would have liked to experience a life other than that as Ray's wife, but she never verbalized it. I could tell by the way she listened to my stories of SoHo or Lisa's stories about DC.

"Good timing," Mase added. "I need to talk to Ray anyway."

It struck me as odd that Mase would be friends with Ray. On the surface it didn't appear that they had anything in common. Ray was uneducated and gruff, and a little scary. Mase was sophisticated in a non-snobby, likable way. They'd been friends since grade school when their families had lived in the city. Ray's family had moved into the house next door so his dad could get a job at the new auto plant. They spent summers at camp together, and they both roamed the neighborhood causing havoc and doing what little boys do. Their lives took different paths when Senator Downes was elected and Mase went to college, and Ray went to work at the plant.

I wanted to stop and see Leese on our way, even though it really wasn't on the way. I tried to stop every day after work, even if it was just for a minute, to let her know I was there and to see if she had made any improvement. I had missed the past two days because of everything that had been happening, and it made me feel like I wasn't prioritizing her like I should. Mase waited for me with the kids in the car, and reminded me, nicely, to make it quick.

"Hey girl, how's your people?"

"Excellent. Yours?"

"You know, the boy is always in trouble but the girl's got a nice fella."

The ladies at the nurse's station knew me and were generally very pleasant whenever I came by. Some I got to know well enough to ask about their kids sincerely and not as a matter of politeness.

"Can I go in, Miss Lou?" I asked as I walked by her desk, as more of a formality because they let me come and go as I pleased.

"You go right ahead, darlin'," she said.

"Thanks," I said, already opening the door to Lisa's room.

It looked the same as it always did, except there was

a ray of sunlight streaming through the window across her face. She looked like a child and the sun made it look like her face was radiating gold light. I kissed her on the cheek like I always did and slid the chair that was next to the wall up to her bed. She was still breathing on her own.

I took her hand in mine.

"Hi, Leese. It's me. Got the fam downstairs in the car. Mary Sue called, and wants us to come over. Isn't that weird? Out of the blue and on a Sunday."

Her chestnut curls framed her face in a way that mirrored her resemblance to AJ. It was unquestionable.

"You better go then," she whispered.

I was stunned.

"Leese," I said softly, leaning toward her face. I needed to make sure I wasn't hearing things, "did you say something?"

I stared at her mouth. She barely moved her lips, but clearly said, "You better go then."

"Oh my God! You are awake! Oh my God!"

I ran to the door, flung it open, remembered I was in a hospital and contained myself, barely, as I ran to the nurse's station.

"Miss Lou, Miss Lou! She's awake! She spoke to me. Lisa spoke to me!"

"Oh Lordy, girl," she said and tried to jump to her feet. She was probably around sixty-five or seventy years old, with white and gray hair in a beehive and was wearing a white dress, and white orthopedic looking shoes. I followed her into the room as she clomped toward Lisa and stood next to her as she took Lisa's hand in hers.

"Lisa, honey, can you hear me?" she said.

There was no response.

"Lisa, can you hear me, dear?" she repeated loudly.

"No need to yell," Lisa whispered, her eyes still closed.

"Sorry, honey," she said. "Can you open your eyes?"

Just then, Mase entered the room.

"Come on, Lanie, we need to go. The kids . . ."

I held my hand out with my finger up to shush him before he could finish.

"Lisa's awake!" I loudly whispered and motioned him over.

He came to my side right away and put his hands on my shoulders while we waited with anticipation to see if Lisa would respond to Miss Lou's commands.

Slowly, Lisa opened her eyes. Her lids fluttered a little and then it looked like she was purposely squeezing them open and shut—like she was trying to focus.

I looked at Mase and before I could say anything, he took off. I knew he read my mind and was going to get AJ.

"Leese, can you see me?" I asked, squeezing her hand and leaning almost directly over her.

"I can certainly hear you," she whispered softly and smiled. "And yes, I can see your gorgeous face."

Miss Lou left to get a doctor, and I just stood there smiling and crying.

"Oh my God, Lisa," I sniffled.

I sat on the edge of her bed and held her hand to my cheek. "I thought we might lose you."

She smiled and barely turned her head toward me. "AJ?" she whispered.

"He's fine, love. He's more than fine, he's fantastic.

Mase just went to get him for you."

She closed her eyes again and we both breathed deeply.

Miss Lou came in and reported the doctor was on his way, and she began taking note of Lisa's blood pressure, respiration, and pulse.

After what seemed like an extraordinarily long period of time, Mase appeared with AJ.

"What took so long?" I asked.

"He was stinky," Zoey chimed in.

Mase handed the baby to me and I leaned over to whisper in Lisa's ear. "Would you like to meet your son?"

Once more she slowly opened her eyes.

I held him above her face, far enough back so she could get a full view but positioned so she wouldn't have to move her head to see him.

"Leese, meet your son. AJ, this is your mama."

He was cooing and drooling and smiling.

Lisa smiled and her eyes watered. Tears streamed down her cheeks.

I lowered the baby down onto her stomach and reached under the blanket for her arm, which I positioned over his back. She was obviously very weak, but I wanted her to feel him.

I felt the salty wetness of my own tears as they pooled in the corners of my mouth. I noticed Mase was trying to remain composed himself.

About that time, Zoey pushed her way up to the side of the bed. "Hi, Aunt Leese," she said, looking around and assessing the situation.

Before Lisa could even attempt to acknowledge her, Zoey said, "Your nails really need some work."

"I know, girlfriend, I know," Lisa whispered to her.

The doctor entered and stopped suddenly as it was clear he didn't expect this ruckus.

"Okay," he said, "I need to examine my patient and she needs to rest. Party's over."

I was too happy to be annoyed at his necessary intrusion.

I held AJ's cheek next to Leese's so she could feel him and smell him, but the doctor's look said we needed to wrap things up, so I didn't delay.

I leaned over and kissed her on the cheek. "I love you and we'll be back tomorrow."

Mase followed with a kiss, and then Z.

By the time we were all situated in the car, I had completely forgotten about Mary Sue's call.

"I texted her we'd be late and why," Mase said, as he finished strapping in AJ.

I climbed into the passenger seat of the truck, sat back and enjoyed the beautiful early afternoon, the kind between fall and winter when the temperature is perfect and you can smell the change of the season in the air. Life was good and Lisa was awake. I felt as if I was radiating joy.

Chapter 23

Our thirty-minute drive to Ray's included several dirt roads canopied with overhanging tree branches. Most still had their leaves, surprising to me in late fall. We sang songs along with the radio, and I was glad for the Patsy reprieve. When we finally turned into their driveway I was relaxed and hungry.

"Holy cow!" I exclaimed.

"Wow," Mase added.

Zoey stretched as far forward as her seatbelt would allow to see what we saw.

"That looks pretty bad," she offered.

Off to the right of the drive as we pulled closer to their house we saw Ray's camo Ford, with the front end smashed in and tree branches coming out of the hood. The windshield was cracked on the driver's side and one of the big, oversized tires on the front were flat. We emerged from our truck and walked around Ray's "oohing" and "aahing" and pointing, like it was an exhibit at a local zoo.

"Damn, he just got those tires," Mase said. "And look at all the dirt in the radiator."

"Mom, look." Zoey pointed toward the back of the truck.

I followed her direction and saw a broken beer bottle sticking out of the back tire. How was that even possible?

Sundays were usually recuperation days in

Banjoland, and by the look of Ray's truck, there was probably major recuperation happening.

I had a pretty good idea of what happened to Ray's truck, even without an explanation, because weekends in Banjoland were fairly predictable. A gathering would take place, probably a tractor pull or cookout—the event itself didn't really matter because whatever was happening was just an excuse for fellowship and drink. Sometimes, most times, nothing of significance resulted from these gatherings other than an irrational argument or two. But there were times, and this was clearly one of them, that things got way out of hand.

Mary Sue appeared in the doorway and came out to greet us, wiping her hands on her bright floral apron. There was no sign of Ray.

After a traditional side hug she explained what happened. Scotty Mac McCutchin had just bought a new dark green Toyota T-100. Ray was very proud of the old Ford he had modified over the years. Seems that the only way to determine which was more powerful was—in their neck of the woods—to race. As I recreated this scene in my mind, I pictured the collective all gathered, women and children off to the side making comments about all the "foolishness" of their men while secretly hoping theirs would win. The men would be holding cans of Busch Light and debating the merits of each truck like they were professional analysts.

Mary Sue was in such a tense and aggravated mood, and I wondered why she'd asked us here.

"Where's Ray?" Mase asked, while Z and RJ tinkered with his 4-wheeler.

"Left about an hour ago," she said. "Got a call from one of the senator's people. Said he had to take care of some business and he'd be back later."

Mental Note – it seems everyone has some kind of relationship with Senator Downes and I'm becoming convinced it was him—likely his people— who trashed my house. Rather than go home to SoHo, I'm now feeling like I want to jump all in figuring out what's happening. I've got a second wind.

"Did he mention that he was supposed to meet me here?" Mase asked her.

Her reply was smothered with contempt.

"Honey, he was so hung over he could barely put his pants on. It's likely he forgot all about meeting you."

Mase took out his phone and tapped on the screen.

"He needs rehab," Mary Sue said bluntly.

In the last year alone, Ray had wrecked the truck once before, been stopped for speeding, and avoided a DUI because the senator intervened on his behalf. And then there were the stupid arguments with anyone who disagreed with him. It was safe to say that even the most casual observer would agree that Ray had a drinking problem.

But that's not why I asked you to come over," she continued. "I'm going to divorce him and I'll need your help with RJ."

This truly surprised me because she had endured him for so many years. Maybe her longing for a different life gave her the motivation to do it, but this was just my guess.

"I'll be happy to help, of course, but are you sure this is the answer?"

"Honey, I've never been more sure of anything in my life."

****

The Wine and Swine Festival. I almost forgot. The atmosphere as Mase had described it reminded me of hometown USA. His mouth literally watered as he described the crispy fried chicken, desserts atop red-checkered tablecloths, the secret recipes prepared for the judges by the matriarch of each family.

We wandered around the "Fest" as the locals called it, holding hands, pushing AJ in a stroller and looking at the various vendor booths. Z stopped to chat with anybody and everybody. We were in the "in-between" time of year, no longer sweltering during the day, but not yet gray and cold. Late autumn was gorgeous, and the leaves were in their glorious vibrant fall colors. Mostly oranges and yellows in the Deep South.

Zoey was looking for the booth where she could toss the Ping-Pong balls into the goldfish bowls, determined to prove she could win a fish.

I was, dare I say, feeling happy in the moment.

"Come on! Come on!" RJ exclaimed, elbowing his way through the crowd and stopping briefly in front of us. "I don't want to be late—I'm going to catch the pig."

Mary Sue rolled her eyes at the dramatic presentation from her son and motioned to Zoey to come along with them. "Don't you want to try and catch the pig, honey?

"No, ma'am," she replied without hesitation. "Mingling with pigs is not for me, and besides, I'm not dressed for it."

As this was the main event of the Wine and Swine Festival, we followed the Jenkins to their reserved seating at the top, center, of the bleachers. We had a good view of the muddy pen and of the people walking around the festival grounds.

Five pigs of various sizes and shapes were covered in some kind of grease, and three hosers—teenage boys—kept the pen muddy. Boys and girls were segregated by age, and the youngest children lined up just inside the gate to listen to the pigmaster announce the process.

"Okay, boys and gals, you know the rules. The first one to catch the pig and hold him until I get there is the winner. There will be no pushing or shoving. And the winner will get …"

"The golden pig!" they shouted in unison.

The golden pig, a gold-plated replica of a female hog (with an apple in its mouth) mounted on a plaque had been passed around since the first festival, circa 1898, and spent the year in the winner's home until the next festival.

Ray appeared from somewhere under the bleachers and gave RJ final instructions before he walked off and disappeared into the throng of people milling about. Mase offered me a quick peck and said he had to meet Smitty and he'd be back shortly.

"On your mark, get set, go!" the pigmaster bellowed, and with that, a full-grown pig was released from the barn into the pen.

RJ was in the center of the pack, but the pig seemed to be in control, running at least four or five child steps ahead of the mob. After about ten minutes, children started falling back.

I laughed at the sight of these little mud-covered children, their parents cheering like it was an Olympic event. The children's faces were so red they looked like chocolate-covered cherries. RJ was still in the hunt, but he didn't look like he had much energy left.

At last, a small chubby boy fell on top of the pig and they both lay in the mud, breathing heavily. The pigmaster made his way over to the little boy and raised his hand like they do in a prizefight. RJ ambled over to us, and while Mary Sue was wiping the mud off his face with a small pack of purse tissues, we heard a large, deafening explosion boom from directly behind us. It sounded like a cannon and it rocked the bleachers so intensely that I was barely able to hang on to AJ, who had been napping on my shoulder. In what seemed like one unified motion, everyone turned toward the direction of the blast to see what we could. Children were screaming and people were scrambling all around us.

"Holy cow!" Zoey exclaimed.

Flames were shooting through the roof of an old horse barn that fortunately was now being used to store tractors and equipment, I heard someone say. It looked like the left side was blown off and random pieces of wood were on fire and strewn across the tall grass.

Thick smoke billowed out of a shattered window and hung over the barn like fluffy black marshmallows. While we were staring at the flames and what was left of the barn, another smaller explosion occurred that blew pieces of the roof in every direction. It was a spectacular site, scary and powerful. After a brief minute to assess the situation, several men began running toward what was left of the structure.

Before they made it to the building, we saw a silhouette against the flames walking toward us.

It only took a split second for me to recognize Mase stumbling across the field. I handed AJ to Mary Sue and took off running behind the men who had seen him first. They enveloped him and put his arms around their shoulders. I was filled with love and fear and panic.

I reached them in record time. Mase's face was smudged with soot and he smelled like smoke. He had a cut on the top of his right hand that was bleeding a little bit, and his shirt was torn across the front.

"Mase," I said, panting heavily, "are you okay?"

"I think so," he said, grimacing a little. "I twisted my ankle trying to run, but I'm okay I think."

"What happened?" I asked.

"I don't really know," he said, turning to look at the destruction behind him.

He was clearly shaken and disoriented.

He refused to go to the emergency room, opting to go home instead. His phone rang non-stop all the way to the house, and he talked in veiled, short answers. Once we got home and situated the kids, I turned on the TV and waited impatiently for an explanation. Mase sat on the couch next to me rearranging a washcloth I had brought him filled with ice, on his ankle. He looked sunburned and stressed.

Before he could utter anything else, footage from the Fest showing the burning barn came across the screen with the tagline: "Wine and Swine erupts into inferno. One found dead."

"One found dead?"

I did not know anyone else was in the barn with Mase.

"It was Ray," he said, looking at the TV.

I tried to wrap my head around what this meant.

Tears fell from his eyes. It was obvious he was trying to control himself as he held his hand over his mouth to try and muffle his sobs. I wrapped my arms around his shoulders and held him tightly for a few minutes until he regained control. I kissed him softly on the cheek and when I looked up, Zoey was standing naked in the doorway.

"Mom, I'm all pruny. Too much time in the tub is not good for a girl's skin."

I kissed Mase on the head, and whispered, "I love you and I'll be right back."

While I was blow-drying Z's hair and she was rambling on about compost and going green, I thought about Mary Sue and RJ and what this meant for their lives. Then I thought about Ray. And where was Smitty? And why was Mase in that building

These were just some of the questions that were percolating in my mind as I tucked Z into bed, and she read me the latest made-up adventure she created from her tablet.

When I returned to the living room and sat down next to him, he was on the phone, much more composed.

"What do we know?" I asked him.

"I'm trying to figure that out," he said.

I scrolled through my phone while he texted and made some calls.

Finally, he spoke. "I lied to you, Lanie, and I'm sorry." He rested his hand on mine.

"What do you mean you lied? About what?"

"I wasn't meeting Smitty, I was meeting Ray. I approached him a few weeks back, before I was taken off the case, to try and see if he knew anything that might be helpful to us since he did work in some capacity for my father, "but at that time he told me 'no' and I accepted that as truth. Then last week he got into it with my dad, who told him he was making a fool of himself with all his drinking and shenanigans and that he would no longer be part of his team—that's what he likes to call the people that work for him. His team. Ray was pissed and decided that he might have some information that would be useful to us after all."

"So you lied?"

"Ray said not to let anyone know we were meeting, and it just seemed the easiest explanation, but I was going to fill you in once I knew if he had any information of value."

"Why didn't you just give Smitty the info and let him follow-up?"

I knew the answer as soon as I asked the question.

"Because Ray doesn't trust anyone who works for the government, except for me and that's because he has known me for most of my life."

I listened intently.

"When we went by his house after we saw Lisa, he was supposed to give me whatever information he was going to give me. Mary Sue texting you made the meeting that much easier. Before we showed up, my father called and asked him to come over for a discussion. That's the term he uses for all his meetings, '"discussions."' Ray texted me when he realized he wouldn't make it in time to meet me and we agreed to follow up at the Fest."

I nodded.

"Lanie, I'll never forget what I saw." He paused for a moment. "I opened the door on the back side of the barn because we had agreed to meet inside, since no one would have any reason to be in there and we wouldn't be seen together by my father while he was politicking at the Fest. I stood in the doorway for a minute so my eyes could adjust to the dimness inside. Ray was standing about twenty-five feet in front of me. The sun shining over my shoulder made his features hard to distinguish and cast a distorted shadow on the wall behind him. I was only in the doorway for a minute, max, when Ray just exploded in front of me."

He started to sob again but regained his composure quickly. I wasn't sure what "exploded in front of me" meant, and I didn't ask.

"It was like he erupted in flames, and then everything around him erupted in flames. It was hard to tell where it began. It all happened at once."

The visual I had in my mind was detailed and disturbing.

"And..." he hesitated. "What if it was done on purpose?"

That was the question that had been foremost in my mind, among others, but he didn't give me a chance to answer. It was as if he was working out what happened while he was talking to me.

"If someone did this on purpose," he continued, "who would that be and why?"

He rubbed his chin and took a deep breath.

"If my father knew Ray was meeting with me secretly and wanted to stop him, would he do this? And risk killing me, too?"

****

Ray's funeral was held exactly three days to the hour after he died. Mary Sue had been medicated for most of that time and her sisters and mother had immediately taken up residence with her as soon as they heard the news. I had never attended a Southern funeral, and I expected it wouldn't be much different than the traditional Irish wake and funeral customs I was used to.

201

It was.

The service itself was in a country church not too far from where they lived. It was small but comfortable, and I was surprised at the number of people who came. The choir sang old time Gospel hymns, ending with a rousing version of, "How Great Thou Art," which Mary Sue and her decked out friends in oversized dress hats sang along to in the front row, between sobs. The preacher spent the majority of the service scaring the hell out of us and telling us that whenever the Lord called our name, that was it, it was over, there were no more chances. He didn't even mention Ray until he was almost finished speaking, and then said that even though he "backslid" the mercy of our Lord might still save him from the fiery pit of hell. I thought that was a little harsh, and by this point I was contemplating my own salvation. The service ended with an Altar call for anyone that wanted to avoid eternal damnation.

"Come get saved! Avoid God's righteous judgment, brothers and sisters! Do it now, before it's too late!" the minister barked.

It was so dramatic.

"Mom, are we saved?" Zoey whispered, a look of deep concern dampening her sparkly blue eyes.

"Yes," I answered.

"How? How did we get saved?" she asked, "and how much do we have to save to be saved? I don't want to go to the fiery pit of hell, Mom!"

Mental Note: I need to have a discussion with Z about God and religion. Catholic school does not prepare anyone for a service like this one.

I whispered to her little face eager for answers. "God loves all of His children, and that includes you and me and it doesn't matter how much money we save, and we aren't going to end up in the fiery pit of hell."

She seemed relieved for the moment and accepted my explanation, thankfully, or we would have been on our knees at the front of the church with strangers laying their hands on us and praying for our souls and exorcising our demons. I probably needed to limit the amount of time she listened to Reverend Jeremiah P. Johnson.

The other thing that really surprised me—aside from the focus on hell—was the amount of food people brought. We Irish enjoy our food and drink, but this was so overwhelming there wasn't enough room for all of it. Ladies from two different churches brought casseroles and cakes—all homemade— and all from some cherished family recipe. Every single person that stopped by to pay their respects brought food, including us.

Mase appeared to be doing alright and RJ was coping. I think he, like Mary Sue, was still in shock. The senator and Olivia also showed up to pay their respects, him politicking and she dutifully next to him, appropriately interacting but still aloof. Mary Sue had no idea that he could have been involved in Ray's death, but I knew one way or the other, Mase was going to find out.

Olivia allowed herself to be hugged, stiffly, and Mary Sue seemed oddly grateful for the opportunity to do it. Senator Downes tried to discreetly hand her an envelope, but she made such a production about the money inside of it that he was obviously uncomfortable at the attention she was drawing to them. As they stepped backwards towards the door, trying to extricate themselves from her thankfulness, I wondered if he had, in fact, tried to kill his own son.

Chapter 24

The week before the trial was a frenzy. It was the biggest media event to happen in the state in at least a decade—since the government tried to take land owned by old man Peterson "for the good of the nation" because Indian artifacts had been found on it.

Michael DeMarco was on the news almost nightly offering his perspective on the judicial process. I hoped he was paying as much attention to Ad's defense as he was to his public profile. Ad was upbeat and positive now that Lisa was on the road to recovery, but DeMarco said we really needed the ledger or his outcome was very "uncertain."

Mase didn't comment much during this time. He had his own concerns. Adam knew what information the government had against him, and Mase wasn't a prosecutor, but he might have to testify about payoffs and marked money and whom he gave it to and for what purpose. This would make his covert activities known by his father for the first time. This was before they knew where the trail was leading and shortly before Ad was removed from the case. And even though Mase felt justified, this would be the first time he would publicly be identified as a participant in the investigation.

The one who was in the spotlight the most during this time was Senator Downes. He was campaigning and denying any wrongdoing.

"You'll see I'll be acquitted of these egregious charges," the senator would say. "I can't be responsible for those close to me who take advantage of that position. I will see that they are prosecuted to the fullest extent of the law."

Anyone with any sense at all could see that he was setting up Ad. If we only had the damn book.

Our lives were in limbo until we knew what was going to happen with Adam once and for all. Mase was on edge, but as usual, kept his worries to himself.

****

"Smitty told me the forensics report came in today on Lisa's accident," Mase said, as he took off his shoes and loosened his tie.

Smitty was such a loyal friend. He and Mase had been partners since Mase began with the agency and he kept Mase in the loop even though he probably shouldn't have. We'd been waiting for this key piece of information for what seemed like months.

"And?" I said, handing him a beer and plopping down next to him on the couch.

"Latent fingerprints on the glove compartment and the steering wheel match those of one Hototo Maw."

"Who is Hototo Maw?"

"Sunglasses," Mase said, "explains why he is dead."

Sunglasses *was* the S.O.B. who ran Leese off the road.

"Enlighten me."

"We think my father assumed Ad had the ledger and that he would have to get it to his attorney to make a deal. The only person able to bring it to him was Lisa, and he probably had Sunglasses staking her out." He continued, "and when he found out that Lisa was meeting us, he knew that was the time to act—that if she had it, she'd need to get it to Adam."

I nodded.

"So," I said, "he sent Sunglasses to get it from her?"

"Yep," he said.

That would make sense.

"It gets better." He opened his phone to show me some pictures. One was a picture of a small flip phone like Ad had to communicate with Senator Downes.

"Take a look at the last text." He swiped to the next picture. It was a picture of an open text from that phone.

I squinted my eyes to block the glare and read it:

—Me: I have what you want and it will cost.—

—S: Don't fuck with me Tonto. Bring me what's mine.—

—Me: You pay or someone will. Many will want what I have.—

—S: You don't know who you're screwing with!—

"Where did you get this?" I asked.

"Pat found the phone in Sunglasses' things. As soon as the forensics report came back Smitty called him. He wanted Pat to get out to the Reservation before the police did. They would have likely found it, but we, well Smitty, had the advantage of seeing the report before anyone else. Pays to know people in the lab."

The pieces were starting to fit. Sunglasses didn't give the ledger to the senator; he was blackmailing him.

I looked for the date on the text.

"Yep! I knew it!" I said. "Look at the date. It was after my house was trashed. Which means—"

"Which means that my father didn't have the ledger then. Sunglasses sat on it, probably told him that Lisa didn't have it with her. Then my father's flunkies trashed your house looking for it—all the while Sunglasses holding it back, letting my father squirm until he was ready to drop the bomb."

"Which exploded on him." I was glad. Good. "Now what do we do?"

"I think they are going back to the Res to search around some more because Smitty didn't find it when he was out there and found the phone. Meanwhile," he sighed, "I'll be doing desk work."

****

Billy Joe's was the place where everyone liked to hang out, the place where people always stopped to chat and have a beer, and where there was always food. It didn't matter what time of day it was, Sue Ellen always had something ready, or almost ready to eat, and they were very welcoming to everyone, no matter who they were or where they came from—it was the epitome of Southern hospitality and always a fun time.

I thought about how much I appreciated them and their attempt to distract us with this cookout as I drove slowly toward the corner of their cute little brick house for the weekend cookout and pulled into the row of camo trucks that ran perpendicular across the lawn. Mase left before me because, he said, Billy Joe's septic tank "blew up again" and the regulars were going to try to rig up something so they wouldn't have to use the outhouse that was built at the same time as their house, and surprisingly was still usable, instead of the bathroom. I saw an open space next to Mases's truck and pulled in slowly. Off to the side of the house, near the deer skinning shack, I saw a gator hanging from a pole by its tail while the smell of charcoal from the grill filled the air.

"Lanie!"

"Hey, RJ."

"Mason has a surprise for you!"

"Really?"

"Yep, and it's a big one."

Mary Sue appeared out of nowhere.

"Hey, buddy, Zoey's lookin' fer ya," she said, and ushered him away.

"Hey, girl," Mary Sue offered, let's go have a seat by the fire."

"Okay, but tell me, how are you? How's RJ?"

"We're okay," she answered. "Being around everyone helps."

We chatted as we meandered towards the group, and as we approached, someone handed me a welcome refreshment and dragged over a chair for me to have a seat near the firepit. The sun was beginning to set and the temperature was quickly becoming cooler. Zoey and RJ came riding up on his four-wheeler from the pond behind the house, covered in mud.

"Did we miss it?" asked Zoey, out of breath.

"Miss what?" I asked, wiping the mud off her face with my sleeve.

"Your surprise."

"Nope, no surprise yet," I said, as my curiosity piqued.

"Phew!" She climbed onto my lap, mud and all, still uninhibited and cuddly.

Mason came out of the house and handed me an oversize sweatshirt that smelled like Tide, grabbed himself a beer, and kissed me on the cheek. By now I noticed the collective gathering around us. I was peaceful and tired.

"I've been talking with little miss here," Mase began, "about us becoming an official family."

She nodded in agreement, smiling through her mud-crusted lips.

"And so I thought," he said, dropping to one knee and handing Billy Joe his beer, "that I'd make us official tonight."

Mason took a ring with a large diamond (two carats by my quick glance) out of his shirt pocket and slipped it onto my finger.

"Lanie, you know I love you."

I did know.

"And I love Zoey, too." He kissed her on the forehead. "I think we make a great family, and I'd like you to be my wife. Would you, please, be my wife?"

The group went silent in anticipation of my response. I breathed it all in. I looked at the couples, our friends, and their children—each one of them. I smelled the hot coals on the grill and felt the crispness in the air. I saw the gator hanging from the pole by its tail, and this handsome man in front of me.

My last marriage proposal seemed like it happened to someone else. I was a different person now, and I lived an entirely different life. I did love Mason, but what if he changed once we were married? What if he left? What if he wasn't who he really seemed to be? This time, if anything crazy happened, it would affect a little girl and me, and I didn't think I could survive another marital disaster. But I felt peace inside. There was nothing about Mason's character that was the same as Junior's, and I knew it.

I teared up a little. "I'd be happy to be your wife," I answered and leaned in for his tender kiss.

There was applause, and fellowship and celebratory laughter late into the evening.

Chapter 25

The atmosphere outside the courthouse was like a circus. Big vans with huge satellite dishes clogged the streets surrounding the building. Television reporters were jamming their microphones into anyone's face just for a comment, a hopeful snippet of something new to report. Those that were directly involved in the trial were escorted inside through a heavily secured back entrance, where the reporters and news crews were stopped and told there would be no cameras allowed in the courtroom. Ad had identified me as someone to use as a character witness for him if Mike DeMarco thought it would be helpful, so because of that I wasn't allowed to be in the actual courtroom either.

Witnesses for the defense were led to one waiting room and witnesses for the prosecution to another. Senator Downes' trial was scheduled to begin immediately after Adam's, so he wasn't allowed to listen to any testimony and was kept away from the chaos in a makeshift staging area. DeMarco wasn't able to negotiate a plea deal even though Adam agreed to testify for the prosecution against Senator Downes, but he was able to get him prosecutorial consideration, which in my understanding meant they would try to do something to help him out if they could.

The first day ended uneventfully, as it was consumed with procedural motions and rulings, evidentiary questions, and juror issues.

I spent most of the day writing in my journal, the one I started when I first moved to Banjoland and texting Lisa, who was almost ready to be discharged from the hospital. The therapist I saw after Junior's first death suggested writing down my feelings in a journal as a healthy way to express and purge them. I had so many conflicted feelings when I moved down South, I figured journaling would be a good way to handle those feelings as well as document the journey itself. It read like a mini novel.

Mental Note: My life really is stranger than fiction and I have officially begun work on the novel.

DeMarco entered the witness room followed by an aid, and then Ad.

"That was routine," Mike DeMarco said, closing the door behind Ad.

A guard was stationed just on the other side of it.

"Tomorrow will be a little more of the same, and then you're on the stand," he said to Ad.

"Do you remember what we discussed?"

Ad nodded.

They continued to prep for an hour until court ended for the day.

Mase said he and Pat and Smitty and their people had no luck finding the ledger. For all we knew the senator had it. And that made me think of Sunglasses. He crossed the wrong man. I wondered if the senator knew about his escapades with Olivia.

And then it hit me! It came to me from out in left field, but nevertheless, I knew where to look, and I knew I didn't have much time.

****

It was dusky on my drive home from court, and I texted Mase that I would be late. It was his turn to get the children, so I had some time before I would really be missed.

I parked on the construction site just like Lisa did when she was here, and I walked the distance of a few houses before I followed the edge of their brick Tudor into the backyard and along the fence to the gate. There were no lights on, and it didn't look like they were home. Monday was their usual card-playing night at the club with others of their social status, and because of who they were and their need to keep up appearances and the perception of his innocence, they kept their social calendar intact. This was predictable. I slipped inside the gate and as soon as I saw the pool, thoughts of Olivia and Sunglasses came flooding into my mind. She really was a stunning-looking woman. Even naked. I shook that memory for the moment and focused on what to do next. I knew from the times that they were on vacation and Mase had to let in the Help, that there should be a spare key on the windowsill in the pool house.

I quietly made my way to the pool house, got the spare key, and let myself into their home. I could hear my heart pounding as I skulked through the house to the master bedroom, which was an enormous space at the end of a long hallway. I don't know why I hadn't thought about the possibility that Sunglasses may have been collaborating with Olivia before, but now I thought it was a real possibility. And even if they weren't collaborating, it didn't mean she didn't have it now. And if she did, she could hold it over the senator's head and get some revenge for his blatant unfaithfulness and who knows what else? Imagine the irony if she had it here right under his nose. I eased open their bedroom door, but it was difficult to see because not only was it dark outside, but the furniture was also dark wood as well. It was hard to distinguish the darkness from the furniture. I slipped my cell phone out of my pocket to use its flashlight so I could see. I held up the bright light to scan the room. I was looking specifically for one thing.

The first time I was in this house was shortly after Mase and I began dating, when Olivia had organized a supper for the board of directors of the local museum of art, of which she was the immediate past president. Mase was expected to attend. As part of the evening, she did what all Southern hostesses do and gave me a tour of her house. She was already in her late afternoon wine fog and took obvious pleasure in showing me where she kept her jewelry stash—though she tried to be discreet. She simply said that the weight of the stones on her necklace was aggravating a tennis injury and she needed to take it off. She made some exaggerated gestures to unhook the clasp and return it to its place among the others in a large wall safe, which was situated in the master closet behind a portrait of her and the senator. I didn't waste any time wondering why they had a portrait of themselves in the closet, and pulled the picture aside exactly as she did the day she told me that it was "important to keep your valuables secured from the Help." In her process of showing off her jewelry collection, which was spectacular, I noticed she kept some papers in an adjacent compartment.

I remember watching her closely as she turned the dial six audible clicks to the left, then six to the right, and then six back to the left. She did not try to shield me from her task, and I never would've remembered this combination if it hadn't been 666.

By the light of my phone I turned the dial slowly, left, right, left, and pulled on the small rubber handle. It opened with ease. It was at that exact moment that I realized the magnitude of what I was doing. I pushed down the thought that I was looking at serious jail time which was interrupted by blaring banjo music. I was so startled that I panicked and dropped my phone. I frantically grabbed for it and found it between Olivia's Dolces. I quickly pressed the button to vibrate.

"Hello?" I whispered.

"Lanie, is that you? Can you hear me?"

It was Mase.

"Yes. I can't talk now."

"What are you doing? It's getting late."

"I'll explain later. Gotta go."

I hung up, made sure the phone was on silent, glanced around the room and refocused. I faced my phone light back into the safe, breathed deeply, and reached over the jewels to the pile of papers neatly stacked against the shiny back wall. I methodically glanced through the stack. On the top were her passport, some CD's, and bank statements; towards the middle was an envelope with some photos in it. I had to look. There were several photos of people—men and women—in various stages of undress…and naked…and…having sex. I recognized a few. I fought my desire to analyze these closer and continued to ruffle through the stack. No ledger.

Disappointed, I replaced the papers just as I had found them, and as I returned them to their resting place, I felt a lump underneath the felt lining covering the bottom of the safe. I reached along the edge for a slit or cut until I found it. It was about six inches long and I immediately slid my fingers inside and felt the soft leather against my fingertips. I could barely contain my excitement. I removed the prize as quickly as I could and tried to restore things just as I had found them.

I was stuffing everything back into the safe when the closet door slammed open. I whirled around and saw her silhouette taking up the entire doorway. She had a sly smile across her face. For a moment she reminded me of Cruella Deville, minus the cigarette.

"Well, well, what do we have here?" Olivia said with a cockeyed grin, stepping toward me.

I took a step back. I had no words. I was frozen with fear.

"A Yankee thief right here in my bedroom closet," she slurred.

I could smell the sweetness of her last glass on her breath.

I had no idea anyone was in the house—I never heard one sound other than the ones I was making. I was petrified.

"I told my son you were worthless trash. Now he will know for sure."

I did not have words to speak. I didn't know what to do, but I had the ledger in my hand and I wasn't about to let it go. It was all I could do not to pee in my pants.

"What is that in your hands?" she snarled.

I didn't answer as I was planning my escape.

"No words, thief?" she hissed.

She was slurring and stumbled forward, reaching for my wrist.

"What do you have? Let me see it," she said. "The police will need to know what you stole."

She snatched my hands forward and I dropped the ledger onto the closet floor.

We dove for it at the same time, but I used my elbow to block her hand from getting to it before me. She wasn't giving up easily. She pulled my hair and in an almost reflexive way, I backhanded her in the chest. She was swearing and grabbing at me and we were rolling over her designer shoes and getting tangled in her event-specific maxis. The scene was dreamlike, almost unreal, yet happening. Olivia was surprisingly strong, but I was more determined than she was, and I extricated myself from her grip, but not before she scratched my cheek with her French manicured tips.

I stood up, disheveled, and braced myself for her next lunge while I tried to figure out how to get past her. I decided to just go for it and while she was regaining her balance, I pushed her through the door opening. We tripped over each other's feet and I hit my head on her mahogany bed before the rest of me slammed onto the floor. She fell on top of me and pinned my arms with her knees, but she couldn't pry the little book from my hand.

This was bizarre and I felt like I was watching every move each of us made from outside my body.

"Enough of this," she said, breathless but determined. "I will simply call the police."

I began to panic while images of Mase's disapproving face flashed across my mind, with cameos from Z, Lisa, and a host of others. But then, I remembered.

"I don't think you will," I said, suddenly calm.

She chuckled and raised an eyebrow like she couldn't believe I said that as she reached for the telephone on her nightstand. I squirmed out from underneath her and made a dash for my phone, which was still on the closet floor in one of Senators Downes' wingtips.

She glanced in my direction but dialed.

"I'd wait a minute if I were you," I said, as I swiped my phone.

"I don't care what you—" She stopped speaking and slowly lowered the receiver once I opened my phone and showed her the picture.

"Where did you—"

"It doesn't really matter, or does it?" I mused. I closed the screen with the naked picture of her and Sunglasses. "I wonder what the senator would think if he saw it?" His history of cheating notwithstanding, Mase told me there were unspoken rules about such indiscretions. One was that you only chose individuals of your own social status. The fact that she had chosen one of his minions, one that was not white, would cause a scandal of biblical proportions and bring shame upon all of them. Allegedly.

I didn't give her a chance to say anything. I simply returned the phone to my pocket, turned and walked out of her bedroom and down the hallway, ledger in hand. She didn't try to stop me.

****

I was on a high as I pulled into my driveway. I knew Mase was going to be aggravated—I was an hour and a half late. But I had the prize.

I breezed through the front door unable to contain my smile.

"Where have you—" I held out my hand to stop him from finishing.

I didn't speak, instead opting to hold the ledger over

my head like I was holding Simba and presenting him to the villagers in the Lion King.

"Is that…where did you . . .?" He looked confused and surprised.

"You won't believe it," I said, walking to the fridge and pouring some champagne into the flute I always kept chilled. I turned to face him.

"Your mother had it."

I said it like I was reporting the time and temperature.

He looked at me with anticipation and concern, waiting for more of an explanation, and after I took a long sip, I gave him the details. Except the detail of what was in the picture. He didn't push.

"You fought with my mother?" he said, somewhat dismayed.

"Yep. She's stronger than she looks."

I took another drink. In retrospect, I was amazed by it, too.

Mase ran his fingers over the cut on my face and held me close to him. He started to lecture me on the risk I took sneaking into his parents' house, but I guess thought better of it after a minute—I mean it was a moot point now—and followed me to the kitchen table where I placed the worn leather grail between us and opened it to the first page. It read like a who's who of prominent businessmen, politicians, higher ups in the police department, from government agencies in the area, some of whom were on the board at the asylum.

There were several hundred entries from individual and corporations and their off-the-record "donations." A real shocker to me was what the Native Americans paid through their Federal Tribal Fund.

"What do you think this was for?" I asked, pointing to that entry.

"For nothing likely," he said. "But my dad probably told them he would keep any competition, you know, other gambling venues from opening close by as a way to blackmail them."

"And if they didn't pay?" I asked.

"Well, he probably told them since it was now legal, thanks to him and Adam, for other casinos to open close to the Reservation he would encourage it, rather than create obstacles for them, which would mean less revenue for their tribe, fewer jobs, or" he continued, "he just could've threatened them outright and demanded a pay-off."

"I bet this is why my dad had Pat come to the club," Mase added, scrolling through the pages. "Probably to see if he had this book and probably to see what it would take to make sure he kept quiet about whatever he knows."

I pondered this as I sipped champagne. "What now?"

I only asked this question because I thought I should. I knew what I was going to do with the ledger from the minute I got my manicured fingers on it.

"Well," he said, hesitantly, "I can take it from here." He reached for the book.

"No, I don't think so," I said. "I have an idea," and I left before he could stop me.

****

My meeting with the prosecutor in Ad's case didn't take very long.

"It's very simple," I said. "You drop the charges against Adam and I'll give you the gold mine of evidence against the senator you need for a solid conviction."

He really didn't have much of a choice as far as I was concerned. If he said no, I would give it to Mike DeMarco and they would use it in Ad's trial and that would give the senator all kinds of time to prepare a defense, since they would have to let the senator's attorneys examine it as well. If he said yes, he might get the senator to plead guilty to some charges and avoid a long trial, because not only would they have written proof, they would also have Ad's testimony.

I knew they could subpoena me to get the ledger, provided I still had it in my possession, but I also knew that it wasn't really Ad they were after in the first place.

"How do I know you have what you say you have?" Mark Robison, the prosecutor asked, his eyes probing mine.

"You don't," I said, "but once we make an agreement you will," I assured him.

I really did like this feeling of being in the know and of having the power to make something happen, but more than that I liked the feeling of really being able to help my friends. It was just about as satisfying as the look on Olivia's face when I showed her the picture I had saved on my phone.

I knew that once Robison shared information I gave him from the ledger and how it compared to what Adam had told them, plus their other evidence, the DA and everyone would know it was the real deal. He asked to see it, but I knew it would be wise to hold the actual physical book back and not give them the opportunity to just take it. I had it hidden just in case they came searching for it because I wasn't taking any chances. Either we would make a deal or I would give it to

DeMarco, leaving no time for a subpoena.

I got up to leave.

"We just need a couple of days," he began.

"The deal is only for today," I said. That is what Mike DeMarco told me to say when he reminded me that we "never had this conversation" on my way to the courthouse. He gave me a few other pointers as well but cautioned me repeatedly that I was never to say we had spoken.

I could tell Robison was getting frustrated with me. "Wait here," he said tersely, and after several minutes of waiting in his office, DeMarco appeared, and we waited together for Robison's return. After more than an hour, Robison finally materialized.

We were in the hallway outside of his office drinking coffee and speculating when he stepped off the elevator and signaled to us to follow him. He took a seat, shuffled some papers and then looked across his desk to give us the news.

"The judge has agreed to a continuance in Adam's case based on this new information and to allow the prosecution a chance to examine the evidence," he said. After hammering out the details regarding Ad's release, which included wearing an ankle monitor and Ad's affirmation that he would still testify against Senator Downes, DeMarco gave me the okay to turn over the ledger.

"You have to turn it over by close of business today and it has to say exactly what you told us it said," Robison added. "The prisoner is free to go," he told a nearby officer, who I assumed was going to get Ad from the adjacent jail. "You can retrieve him in about an hour," he added.

I hated that he called Ad a prisoner and said we could "retrieve" him. It sounded so impersonal and gruff. It didn't matter, though. Ad was going to be free and get to finally see Lisa. DeMarco and I met him in the lobby of the jail, and he practically sprinted to us as the heavy metal door slammed behind him.

After explaining the details and plan going forward, DeMarco cautioned, "and remember, no contact with the media. No interviews. Lay low."

Ad nodded and we made a beeline for my ride.

"Lanie, I can't believe this!" He hugged me tightly and lifted me off my feet.

I squeezed his hand, unlocked the door, and headed to where I knew we had to go first.

I called Mase as soon as we were on our way to see Lisa.

"You made a deal?" he said. "What about Adam's attorney? There is a way you have to do these things, Lanie."

I laughed.

"I'm serious," he said.

"I know, I know." I chuckled. "Sorry, it's just that we're pretty darn happy. I'm driving Ad to see Lisa and we need you to bring AJ to the hospital, if you would please."

I couldn't help myself; I was giddy with excitement. Ad was out of jail and on his way to see his love, who was awake and getting stronger every day.

"Lanie, would you please tell me what is going on?"

I could hear the frustration in his tone, and so I took a few minutes to fill him in with the details.

"Wow. I guess I shouldn't be surprised," he offered, "I'll bring the kids."

I got to the hospital in good time, extra careful not to break any laws. Ad ran up the stairs and down the hall to Lisa's room. I took my time and waited around the nurse's station for Mase and the children to show up.

"Hi, Mom," Zoey chirped. "Look, Mase did my nails."

She held out her fingernails covered in gold and silver glitter for me to examine. I could see the Elmer's glue underneath it.

"Is that glue and glitter?" I asked skeptically.

"Don't fall to pieces, Mom. We're just trying something new," she said, holding her nails up for all to see—the Patsy Cline reference aside.

After a few minutes, Ad emerged from the room. He hugged me again, gave Z a hug and proceeded to take AJ out of Mase's arms.

"Thanks, man," he said. "I mean it."

"No problem," said Mase, and handed over the baby.

Ad kissed his son on both cheeks and retreated into Lisa's room with us trailing behind.

Lisa was looking so much healthier. She could move her arms and legs, and she could speak softly, and the color had returned to her skin. On the road to a full recovery is what the doctors told us. A miracle they said. She begged me for donuts on my daily visits, and occasionally I would oblige, but I kept reminding her of her own words "carbs equal running." And we both hated running.

Seeing the three of them together for the first time as a family was a little overwhelming for me. I took the opportunity to get a few phone pics, which I knew she would regret not having, and I stood back a little with

Mase to reflect on how our lives had brought us to this point.

"You did good," he whispered in my ear.

"I did, didn't I?" I whispered, smiling back at him.

There was only one thing left.

Chapter 26

It didn't take long for word to get out that Adam had been released, and the media were all over him for some comment or, ideally, an interview. Senator Downes was confused, as anyone might imagine, and summoned Ad to meet with him. No one thought that was a good idea except for the federal prosecutor, who thought Ad should wear a wire to get as much information as possible as he could from a meeting. Mike DeMarco expressly forbade him from doing it. If the senator was responsible for Ray's death, and Sunglasses' for that matter, what would stop him from trying to hurt or kill Ad, the guy that everyone knew was going to testify against him?

Fortunately, common sense—or Lisa—prevailed, and he dropped the idea of a meeting completely. That didn't stop the senator's thugs from harassing him about what he knew and that he better remember "who was calling the shots."

Because of the Ad situation and that his charges had been dismissed, the prosecutors petitioned to have the senator's trial date moved forward. The bomb should be dropped any day about the ledger and then the likely offer of a deal, according to Mase, and the fact that they had Pat to testify as to what exactly the money from the Native Americans was to be used for seemed to be icing on the cake. Mase and Ad both reminded us that the senator could still elect to go to trial and take his chances there—and that's exactly what he did. According to Mase and to Mike DeMarco (who was still giving interviews) he felt like his high-powered legal team could get him exonerated.

****

The trial began as Ad's had, a day of motions and filings and legal maneuvering. I was surprised, though I probably shouldn't have been, at Senator Downes' composure. He was the consummate politician, smiling for the cameras and proclaiming his innocence. Mase said not to be surprised if he could buy his way out of these charges against him.

"You know he has connections everywhere, right?" he reminded me.

"You think he's going to get off?" I was ticked off at that thought.

"I'm not saying he will, but if there is any way he can, and I mean any way, he will," Mase said.

No cameras were allowed in the courtroom, but every day there was a summary of what took place and key developments on TV and Online.

The first few days were spent establishing relationships, both with people and responsibilities. Mase had been on the witness list for the prosecution because of evidence (bribes and recorded calls) he had been responsible for obtaining, but Mark Robison felt like they had enough evidence without using him, and frankly, had been open about not wanting the frenzy from the media this would have caused from the whole "son testifies against father" angle. Not compromising the investigation was the major reason Mase was reassigned once evidence pointed to his father to prevent any appearance of impropriety. There didn't seem to be the slightest concern for Mase's family relationships whatsoever, just the circus this would cause with the media and whether the prosecution could use it to their advantage.

Everything hit the fan the day that Ad testified. Robison and DeMarco had prepared him the best they could, and the prosecution had built a methodical case culminating with the testimony of him and Pat, and the production of the ledger (which the prosecution had to let the senator's defense team know they had). I thought it would be a good idea to be with Leese on this day, and I knew that we probably would not get any news from the courthouse until after lunch.

The doctors told us that Lisa should be able to be discharged from the hospital in a week or so, and that her prognosis was excellent. She would still have physical therapy and speech therapy for a while, but overall things were exceedingly good considering what happened and that she had been unconscious for so long. I was grateful. I don't know what I would've done had she died.

"I can't believe you fought with Olivia to get the ledger," Lisa said. She reached over to touch the scab on my cheek. It was almost gone, but I expected it to leave a small scar. I slid onto her bed like I normally did on a visit and cozied up next to her and set the boiled eggs and dry wheat toast she requested—a sure sign she was getting back to herself.

"I know. It's crazy when I think about it."

"Bitch," we said in unison and then were quiet for a while.

Lisa spoke first.

"What do you think will happen to the senator?" she asked.

I reached across the rumpled covers and took her hand in mine. I rubbed her soft fingers with my thumb.

"I really don't know," I said. "I hope he gets what he deserves."

"Adam says they have a lot of evidence against him," she said hopefully.

"Well . . ." I chose my words carefully. "He has a lot of money and knows a lot of people."

I felt the need to protect her feelings, which was a reversal of the parameters of our relationship. She was always the one protecting me from something, someone, or most likely, myself. Coming so close to losing her gave me clarity and a sense of fierce protectiveness. I did wonder what would happen if Senator Downes was exonerated, what that might mean for Ad and for Mase. For all of us. I hadn't forgiven Ad for his betrayal, but I knew eventually I would and right now I didn't give my feelings about him a priority given what was happening.

The news from the trial came fast and hard. According to the reports I read on my phone out loud to Leese and the Fox News television coverage, Adam's testimony was torn apart by the defense "bulldog" who "shredded" his testimony one sentence at a time.

God help us.

Another reporter's phrase was a little more palatable when he said the prosecution's witness was "unwavering despite the tenacious attack."

Poor Ad.

There were some good reports, too. Reports that described Ad's composure and relatability to the jury.

****

It was a tumultuous week, with our emotional roller coaster going full speed. When the case finally made its way to the jury, we were spent. It was while we were in the process of taking Lisa home from the hospital that Ad got the call the jury had reached a verdict. After reassuring him that we were okay, he left for the courthouse and Leese and I got comfy at her place. The suspense was almost too much, and we distracted ourselves by letting Zoey paint our toenails. AJ's, too.

All the local TV channels and some national stations showed scenes of the courthouse and interviews with random pundits offering their thoughts. FOX News had a ticker across the bottom of the screen that said: "Jury has verdict in the Wes Downes corruption trial. Stay tuned." It was like there was nothing else happening in the world except this trial. Mase had shown up shortly after us, and was on the porch smoking a cigarette, something I hadn't seen him do before. All of this was overwhelming. I could only imagine how Ad felt, and Mase too, but differently. It was his father on trial and even if they were not close, he must have had some feelings about all that was happening. He didn't talk about it much.

The judge decided to allow cameras in the courtroom for the verdict, so we had a front row seat from Lisa's couch. Cameras panned the room. The jury was seated, and we got to see each juror's face, along with the judge, the attorneys and Ad. Olivia was in the first row dressed for the cameras, and the senator was seated between his attorneys, two well-known defense counselors from Washington, DC whose names were familiar. Senator Downes looked relaxed while he waited for his fate, but for us the anticipation was tangible.

We didn't speak as we watched the judge call the

courtroom to order. After a few minutes, he opened the small piece of paper that the bailiff handed him. Leese, Mase and I held hands, ready for this nightmare to finally be over. All we needed was the formality.

The judge spoke, "Ladies and gentlemen of the jury, have you reached a verdict?"

We leaned forward on the edge of the couch, gave each other a knowing glance, and clinked our champagne glasses hoping for justice to be served.

"Here we go," she said softly.

"Yes, your honor," the foreman said.

"What say you?"

"We find the defendant, Mason Westhoven Downes III... not guilty of all charges."

I dropped my glass to the floor. Leese gasped and her eyes filled with tears. Mase pinched his lips together and shook his head slowly.

The courtroom erupted with shouts; some were cheering, some were shouting angrily. The Native Americans from the Res sat in stunned silence. Senator Downes and Olivia put on a show for everyone, cavalierly laughing and hugging.

The judge tried to reestablish order, but it was difficult. The cameras were fixated on the Downes. It was a circus. He slammed down his gavel repeatedly, yelling "order!" until, with the bailiff's assistance, people returned to their seats. Even the talking TV heads were quiet. Finally, it was calm.

"Will the defendant please rise?" the judge said.

Senator Downes and his attorneys stood up. I guess this was the official you're-free-to-go speech.

How could this be happening?

Leese held her head in her hands, quietly sobbing.

As the judge thanked the jury for their service, Smitty entered the courtroom and walked down the aisle between spectators to the table where Ad and Mike DeMarco were sitting silently. He handed DeMarco a small cell phone, whispered something in his ear, turned and walked out of the room without another word. The counselor appeared to play with the phone for a minute before sliding it over to Mark Robison and the assistant district attorney. They spoke quietly for a moment and then Robinson rose from his seat.

"Hang on ladies," Mase said. "It isn't over just yet."

We refocused.

"What?" we said.

"Watch."

"Your honor," Robison said, "may I approach the bench?"

Senator Downes' attorney objected vigorously on the grounds that the verdict had been given, but the judge called them both forward anyway. It was like watching an episode of *Law and Order*. Both prosecutors approached the judge—Mike DeMarco trailing behind.

Robison handed the judge the phone, which he opened and swiped. He appeared to study the screen for a few minutes and then handed it to the senator's attorney. There was some initial conversation among them and then the senator's attorney and Robison got into it. They raised their voices and were openly arguing with one another. The judge slammed down his gavel and told them both to be quiet. Robison immediately became silent, but the senator's attorney started arguing with the judge. This was unlike any law drama I'd seen before and for a minute I was surprised they kept showing it on TV until I realized how interesting and newsworthy it was.

Leese and I exchanged glances as the scene escalated into the judge shouting at him.

"Stop speaking now or I'll hold you in contempt," he barked to the senator's lawyer.

It was obvious he meant business. It was also obvious that the attorney had more to say and that he was struggling to remain quiet, but he did restrain himself.

The judge continued, "Based on new information, the senator will be remanded into custody immediately until a bond hearing can be scheduled."

The courthouse erupted again and the look on Senator Downes' face could only be described as shock. He was stunned and looked to his people for an explanation. I think Leese and I were just as shocked.

"What the?" she said.

"I have no idea," was all I could say.

Mase's phone rang. "Excuse me," he said, and he stepped out onto the porch.

I sat back on the couch thinking about what we saw and trying to make sense of it all. Lisa went to check on AJ.

"Bet you're wondering what all that courtroom stuff was about," Mase said as he stepped in from the porch and as Lisa returned with the baby.

He had an odd grin on his face as a familiar voice came over his phone speaker.

"Can everyone hear me," the voice asked.

We nodded.

"I know my father," Mase said, "and I know what he's capable of…and I had a hunch."

We didn't interrupt, anxious for details.

"And so I called someone I could trust."

Smitty's voice came through the phone loud and clear.

"We knew that the senator wouldn't leave anything to chance," Smitty said, "and we, thanks to your husband, were tipped off to a cabin on the edge of the old Cullman Plantation when we put him under surveillance a few months ago. It is burrowed deep into the woods and it's difficult to find, and Mason told us only a few of the senator's inner circle were aware of its existence. I staked it out for weeks, and long story short, I got him on video with my phone getting out of a truck we did not recognize with the jury foreman and disappearing inside. I had to get it authenticated and couldn't get that done in time to get to court before the verdict."

I needed a few minutes to absorb this. Lisa nodded her head up and down like it all made sense. She swallowed what was left of her drink in one gulp.

"Aren't you surprised he was this careless?" I asked the phone.

"He wasn't careless," Mase interjected, "he was confident. He didn't realize anyone outside of his immediate circle knew where to find the cabin because he never went there unless he needed to be super covert. I don't think Adam even knew it existed."

We were quiet as we thought about the impact of what he said.

"Don't you feel badly at all, Mase, I mean, he is your dad?

"Of course, but right is right and wrong is wrong, and his actions affect people I love."

I thought about how black and white this seemed to be for him, even when it involved family, like emotions and feelings didn't matter, only what was right.

Mase gave me a quick kiss, and an "I gotta go meet Adam, but we'll be back later to celebrate" as he dashed out the door, still on the phone and leaving me to rehash these events with Lisa.

****

Lisa slowly sipped on a sweat tea, while Zoey fed AJ and we waited for Ad and Mase on her porch. It was an evening like most this time of year, but it had been a day unlike any other. Lisa was finally home, the circus of Ad's trial was over for now, and it looked like justice would eventually be done. I was ready for things to feel like before. Before Junior and the accident, before the search for the little leather book, and before the trial. When life in Banjoland was, dare I say, somewhat normal. I smiled at myself for thinking that Banjoland was now my normal.

"I hope we can get back to. . ."

"Normal," Lisa said. "I know. Me, too. Don't speak to soon."

She looked so much like herself; it was almost as if she had never been in the hospital—

her healing cuts and bruises disappearing more each day.

"Can you believe everything that happened?" she said.

"It'll all be in my book," I joked.

Mase and Ad came racing down the dirt road in Ad's truck, music blaring. They skidded into the driveway amid a cloud of dust, all smiles.

"Hey, ladies," Ad said, strolling across the porch to kiss Leese.

Mase followed from the back of the truck with two fresh beers for them.

"Hey, sexy lady," he growled into my neck.

They were almost jubilant.

"So?" Leese and I said in unison, as usual. We needed details.

Ad nodded toward Mase.

"Well, here's the deal," Mase said. "With this turn of events, the entire case can be retried—with an additional charge of bribing a juror—and they think that there might be more than one, or he can make a plea deal. He could get jail time simply for tampering with the jury, not to mention bribery, extortion and everything else."

Ad was ecstatic and who could blame him. He and Lisa and all of us had certainly been through the ringer during this entire process, especially with Lisa's near-death crash.

"And," Ad continued after taking a large swallow of his Busch Light, "Robison is certain he can get a conviction on the bribing charge because once the foreman saw the video, he admitted to it so he could make a deal! Can you believe it?"

"Finally," Leese said, and sighed into Ad's chest.

Things certainly seemed hopeful, but I knew by now that nothing was ever really as it seemed, and I wondered if it was over. Really over.

Chapter 27

The senator's trial was quick. The defense did their best to come up with a plausible reason for the juror to be with the senator during the trial, but it was not possible, especially with the former juror's testimony. He was convicted and sentenced in the 10 days following his initial acquittal. Shortly after his sentencing Mase received a package from Olivia—more specifically from her lawyer.

"That is odd," he said, as he set the box on the counter with the rest of the mail. "Why would she send me a package?"

He peeled back the brown wrapping.

"That looks like," he interrupted me before I could finish as he examined the contents, "a flash drive," he said. "It is."

We scoured the house for Z's laptop and took our seats as Mase hit play.

The recording opened with Olivia of the Atlanta Westhovens sitting on a chaise, legs crossed, wine glass in one hand, cigarette in the other, mountains in view through an open window. She was wearing one of those designer dresses, high heels, the whole bit. She began, "greetings Mason and Melanie, as you may have guessed by the majestic mountain view behind me, I am in Andorra." I knew she vacationed a lot in that small country, but I still didn't understand this announcement made by flash drive. We didn't have to wait long for an explanation. She continued, just like she was conversing with a friend at the Club and confessed to killing Sunglasses. Before I could figure out why and why she sent this information to us, she explained that he was blackmailing her. He had evidence of their affair and expected her to pay to keep it quiet. What she said next surprised me more. "I told your father everything."

Mase hit pause and explained before I could ask.

"Image is very important to my parent's generation," he said. "Image and secrets, the glue that holds a Southern marriage together," he chuckled, "but don't worry, that's old school—it won't be that way with us," he winked and squeezed my hand, and then continued, "the fact that Sunglasses was not white, would have caused such a scandal that she had to get his help to stop it from becoming public."

"So, it wasn't the affair per se, it was with whom that was the issue." That made sense.

He hit play again. When the recording finished we were stunned, and we sat quietly for a few minutes before Mase said "she knows him very well. If he finds out I told Smitty about the cabin, he might try to blackmail me to do who knows what and if I don't, threaten to expose her crime as a way to get me to comply. Andorra is a country between France and Spain that has no extradition treaty with the United States, so she just has to wait out the statute of limitations before she comes home and then it can never be held over my head, or hers for that matter."

She did love him. In her way, she did, and my feelings about her changed with that revelation, and that extraordinary gift to Mase and our family. Obviously she was protecting herself, too, but she and Downes had so much dirt on each other I could only imagine what would happen if they opened that Pandora's box. They had never exposed each other's deeds before, but the senator had never gone to prison before. These were different times. And now, maybe with the senator going to prison and Olivia "off the continent," maybe we could breathe. Maybe there would be peace. Maybe.

A word about the author…

Kim has always been a storyteller, and after moving South and raising her children, she took advantage of the fertile opportunities surrounding her life in the Deep South to pen her first full-length novel. The contrast in lifestyle from her childhood in upstate New York to that of rural Southern life afforded her many opportunities to broaden her perspective on the different meanings of American life. She currently works in the "City" and returns every evening to life on her farm with her husband and mandatory dog.

Thank you for purchasing
this publication of The Wild Rose Press, Inc.

For questions or more information
contact us at
info@thewildrosepress.com.

The Wild Rose Press, Inc.
www.thewildrosepress.com